Welbore St. Clair Baddeley

Bedoueen legends and other poems

Welbore St. Clair Baddeley

Bedoueen legends and other poems

ISBN/EAN: 9783744722841

Printed in Europe, USA, Canada, Australia, Japan

Cover: Foto ©Andreas Hilbeck / pixelio.de

More available books at **www.hansebooks.com**

BEDOUEEN LEGENDS

AND

OTHER POEMS

BY

W. ST. CLAIR BADDELEY

Member of the Royal Asiatic Society

London

ROBSON AND KERSLAKE

43 CRANBOURN STREET LEICESTER SQUARE

1883

TO MY BROTHER

JOHN F. A. BADDELEY

THESE ALL-TOO-UNWORTHY LABOURS

I send Thee forth as an eager dove,
    In an air that is filled with the sound of strife,
To look for the face of the land of Love,—
    To bring for me hither a leaf of Life.
Bring me a Lotus-flower,—hie with it here,—
That hath pitied the plaint of the waters drear:
For no other flower that breathes can out-last
And league with the flood of the rivers vast;
But this One alone, that is winged as a dove,
And sleeps in the stream, like the spirit of Love,
Aye, this alone, that recloseth to rest
When the sun goes down, in its mother's breast;
And arises fair like a star on the night,
Out of the ripple at morning-light;—
Like a silver roselet outsweetening the Lime;
Like a pearl that may lie on the bosom of Time,
    Like a love-vow kept;—
    Like desire that hath slept;—
Subtle as Love, and chaster than rime!—
    And this to me shall seem Olive and Myrtle,—
    Peace and love and delight therein;
Unhurt by the wearers of Tansy and Whortle
    Who strew Art's ways with a festering Whin!
And This to me shall be Bay-leaf and Laurel,
    Amaranth, too, that doth never fade;
And Thrift and Thyme, and Syringa, and Sorrel,
    With Rose over-laid.

INTRODUCTION.

THE following legends comprise a few of the almost numberless episodes in the life of Antar, the most renowned of Pre-Islamite warriors of the desert ; and are founded on portions of Terrick Hamilton's translation of the ' Romance of Antar.'* The final story of the hero's death is obtained from the Nouveau Journal Asiatique, No. LXIII, where it is translated into French by M. Caussin de Percival.

Though it may be safely affirmed that the noblest figure in Arabian chivalry is almost unknown, even by name, to the general reader, his praise has been sounded in full, if brief, notes, by some of the most illustrious spirits of recent ages. Nothing more pregnant however has actually been uttered concerning him, than the words of Mahomet himself :—
"I have never heard an Arab described whom I should like to have seen so much as Antar ; "—and in another place he says :—" Relate to your children the traditions about Antar : for these will render their hearts firmer than the rocks : " moreover these sayings were spoken by one who was born in the after-glow—when Antar had but lately ceased to breathe. Then there is good reason to believe that

*4 vols. 1825.

the deeds of Antar may have proved an animating example in the eyes of the famous Cid : seeing that the Arabs have continuously been in the habit of reciting them ; and the Moors, with whom he was frequently in contact, and from whom indeed he received his name Scyid or Cid==my lord, were likely enough in possession of the popular classic work of Asmai. Antar receives terse appreciation in later times at the hands of the author of "The Pilgrimage to El Medinah and Mecca," in politest opposition to Eliot Warburton who was brilliant enough not to detect "*any true spirit of Chivalry*" in a man who made and practised the maxim : "Mercy is the noblest quality of the noble ;"—and whose life and death were spent in the defence of the weak and oppressed, as a result of the constant and ennobling passion he entertained for his beautiful cousin Abla.

It is stated in the early part of the translated work that the narrators are Asmai, Toheinah and Abu Obeidah ; the first of whom was a famous grammarian and theologian at the court of Haroun Al Raschid in the ninth century, and to whom alone the honour of the achievement is usually given. The work became augmented in the reign of Khaliph Maimun, and the final edition was published at an uncertain date by Seyid Yusùf-ebn-Ismail. It may be briefly described as a swollen prose-epic. There is much probability however, that under the name and figure of Antar, these authors have related additional typical stories, possibly of more ancient date, and perhaps transposed from other literatures. There are several copies of the

"Romance of Antar" in Europe; the completest being at Vienna; the internal significance of the work nevertheless, has not been grossly closed out by the appalling envelope of 45 volumes; for we have the testimony of the learned Von Hammer that "*this* is the work and *not* the 'Thousand and one nights' (as is generally supposed,) which is the source of the stories that fill the tents and cottages of Arabia and Egypt;"—also Sir William Jones, who first introduced the work into this country, expresses his opinion: "I have only seen the four-teenth volume of this work, which comprises all that is elegant and noble in composition. So lofty, so various, and so bold is its style, that I do not hesi-tate to rank it amongst the most finished poems."

I have thus far spoken of the original work which is the remote parent of the ensuing poems; and I now feel it necessary to say something of the Hero himself, of Abla his spouse, and of the land of his exploits.

Shedàd the father of Antar, and Malik the father of Abla, were illustrious chieftains of the tribe of Bedoueens called Abs. Now it happened that on one occasion these warriors were leagued with eight of their relatives to leave the land of Shurebah on a venturous enterprise—to obtain horses and camels. When they had travelled a great way, they reached the mountains of Aja and Selma, and in an under-lying valley they discovered the wealthy tribe of Jezeela which they were not rash enough to attack: howbe, in passing away from their camp, they came upon the pasturage of their camels, where they be-held a thousand beasts grazing, attended only by a black woman and her two boys. Therewithal they drove off the camels together with their guardian and her children; and although pounced upon, red handed, by a portion of the tribe, they came off successfully, and proceeded homeward till they halted by a stream to divide the plunder.

Shedād, however, was so struck with the loveliness of the woman, that he renounced his rightful share of spoil, and took her to himself instead. Her name was Zebeeba, and the names of her sons, Jerir and Shiboob. In due time she brought forth a third, who though very dark, closely resembled his father Shedād, who was overjoyed at the sight of him, and gave him the name Antar:—more correctly 'Āntără.

Now the youth of Antar, like that of most heroes, from David to Du Guesclin, was distinguished by daring, not to say, fabulous, exploits, which won him an early reputation for strength and valour. He became an excellent horseman: he could throw the reed-spear with a precision almost miraculous: with his staff he slew a wolf that had attacked the flock of his tending: later he killed a slave who had brutally insulted an old beggar-woman in his presence: so that his feats made him an object of wonder and fear. Meanwhile with his physical growth, his mind gave promise of future brilliancy; and whenever a worthy antagonist was to be encountered, Antar addressed him in a fiery lyrical strain which usually became the prelude of victory; wherefore his achievements were the delight or envy of the warriors, and the admiration of the women of the tribe; his beautiful cousin Abla especially used to gather with her maids round him to be charmed by the recital of his adventures.

One day when he brought the milk cooled in the wind (as was his duty being born of a slave-mother) to the tent of his uncle Malik, he saw his aunt combing his cousin Abla's hair, which rippled away down her back,—sable like the river of Night ; but Abla rose, and playfully ran off, displaying its full fragrant wealth to the very ground, and the sight and scent thereof took the eye and heart of Antar in sudden thrall, so that he became anxious and pensive, and thereafter, when he was alone, he broke forth in this manner :

" That fair maid lets down her ringlets, and she is completely screened in her hair, dark as the shades of Night. It is as if She were the glorious Day, and as if Night had covered her. It is as though the full moon was shining in its splendour, and the loveliness of the stars was concealed by its lustre. Her charms bewitch all around her : all are importunate to do her service : they live in her loveliness and assume the colour and sweetness of her graces. O Despise me not for my love of her : for I am distracted, and live but as the victim of my love. *I will hide my passion in my soul till I am fortunate enough at last to serve her.*"

The course of this true Love did not run smooth however ! A turbulent stream of obstacles,—such as jealousies on the part of his uncles, plots of his enemies, and perils of battle,—interwound and interrupted it at every point : yet only thereby did his desire to possess Abla increase. Therefore he sings :—" O Abla, when I most despair, Love for thee, and all its weaknesses, is my only hope." Anon he describes her to himself in a variety of ways : " She moves ; I should say it is the branch of a tamarisk that waves its branches to the southern breeze. She gazes : I should say it is the full moon of the night when Orion girds it with stars. She smiles, and the pearls of her mouth sparkle, which are the cure of a lover's sickness." Then again : " By the truth of my love for thee, my heart can never be cured but by patience ! I will expose myself to every peril, till I exalt myself to the heights of glory with my spear-thrusts and with the blows of my sword : then I shall either be tossed upon the spear-heads or be numbered amongst the Noble."

This last aspiration is an inward reference to the taunt he so often received from his infancy onward, concerning his complexion and parentage. The opportunity at last arrived when the life of Abla and that of her mother was imperilled by the foe : whereupon Abla promised him her hand in marriage if he would save them. Therewith, in the delight of his soul, Antar and his half-brother Shiboob, rushed down terribly '*like the sea when it roars*' upon the enemy, and scattered it in all directions.

Nevertheless, though betrothed to Abla, every obstacle was put in the way of his wedding by the conditions imposed on him by her parents :—such as the acquirement of peculiar dowries, which gave rise to all manner of adventures—a few of which are the bases of the following legends. How Antar, after his return from Persia with enormous treasure from the King of Kings, having finally wedded her, saved her tribe by a heroic death, is the final subject of these verses to which I solicit the Reader's critical good-will.

It is only necessary to mention further, that Antar was the author of one of the seven prize-poems, which, on account of their excellence, were written on Byssus in golden letters, and suspended in the Kaaba at Mecca; and therefore called Mu'allaqāt, or the "Hung-up."

In conclusion I must express my warm thanks to Mr. W. A. Clouston,* and to Mr. E. J. Gibb,† for ever-ready assistance during the progress of this work, and finally to Mr. J. W. Redhouse in regard to the transliteration of certain proper names.

*Author of " Arabian poetry for English readers."   To the kind-ness of this gentleman I also owe the foundation of the Hindu Legend at the end of this volume.

†Author of "Ottoman Poems."

ASYED, son of Jazeema, spent his days
By Zemzem's holy fountain and the Shrine,
Where to himself he drew the things of Light,
To strew them o'er the dark ways of the land ;—
Whereby to quail the weeds of ignorance,
And by sweet virtue summon such delights
As cheer the world and comfort weeping Hope.

Now once a year he left that hallowed place,
And crossed the tedious waste to them of Abs,
To aid his kinsmen by his holy rede,
And swell their pleasures while he shared their teen,—
As is the bounden care of godly men !
Also his brother Zuhayr was their King.

So when the gentle season smiled again,
Bringing the faithful swallow to his courts,
Asyed rose up early ;—kissed the Shrine,
And slowly rode along the silent streets,
Meeting the sunrise thro' the gate of Praise :
Then turning viewed the gardens and the domes
Glittering above the far-off cypress trees,
And all the holy City sleeping, fair ;
While fronting him the dead perpetual plain
Lay stretched in naked desolation there.

B

Three charmèd mornings lit the rippled sand
As he dreamed o'er it, till rare woody sweets
Blew to him,—like the little plumes of song
Loosed in the virgin budding of a grove,—
Heralding far-off vallies : and he sighed,—
" Ah! that those fair days might return once more ! '

What-time the fourth dawn rising o'er the dunes,
Set them aglister like new-fallen stars,
Embossing all the plain,—upon its path
Shining afar came forth the King of Abs
Amid his blithe resplendent chivalry,
Bright as the blossomed Spring : but when he gazed
And marked that mantle dark, that grave demean,
Quitted his steed and passed in front alone,
Charging his knights to meet him in the vale.
So went and kissed his brother waiting him :
Then turning, drew him whence they might descend
Into the vale of Tamarisks, where the deer,
Startled aloof their coverts, tricked the breeze,
Leaving them lingering toward the middle vale.
But when good Asyed saw the dewy trees
Sparkling with soft compulsion secret tears
Rose to his eyes; and thus he cried aloud :—

"O glade of the Tamarisk, where, ah where are the voices
    of Love,
Awake, as they were, like the song of the dove in the hither-
    most leaves ?—
Ah ! say: for my soul yet burns, is my Love still alive in
    the land ?—
I look upon every hand ; the rocks and the trees are the
    same ;
But my heart is a withering flame: for the face that I love
    has flown !
Gone as a leaf that is blown: and no man seems to know

Tho' I am broken with woe !—But all sweet vows that I
    made,—
I have never betrayed: and she to whom they were sworn
Smiled on the light that was born in my face from her
    face when it smiled—
As the starlight smiles on a child upgazing with reverent
    love
From earth to the glories above:—but here am I all alone!
The owls and the ravens are glad in the leaves that belonged
    to the dove ! "

But when he made an end there, kneeling still,
With hands uplift toward the glistening trees
Waving fitfully,—all the gusts of grief
Rushed with replenished storm and tore his soul,
And dashed him prostrate on the yielding sand,
Wailing aloud: " O vale of the Tamarisk-trees,
Where is thy pride,—thy child? O cruel Breeze,
Mocking my hungered soul with all thy sweets,
Ease me of Woe a little !—speak with me !
Tell me of Zenib or Selima,—
Where is my Love—my bride ? "   Now when at first
He knelt him down before the swaying trees,
The gentle King stood marvelling aside,—
Deeming his brother merely offered prayer ;
Or nothing more, despite his quenchless tears,
Than might become devotion, earnest, high ;
But when he saw him fallen thus adown
Imploring to the green insensate trees,
Knew that some tender dole was finding wings,
And bursting from its churlish prison-house :
Therefore he went and softly spake to him,
And raised him in his arms and made him yield
To sweet address, entreating by the Shrine
That he might share the sorrow: so they rose

And wandered on, both Asyed and the King;
Till Asyed wakening to the touch of Shame,
(Which as a father is to trancèd Grief,
Wooing its vanquished breath to vital day,)
By many a coign of speech and tender sigh,
Crept to the darkest hold of his despair—
And thus began: "O Brother, if I speak,
"Adieu the taintless rose of my repute!
"And yet me-thinks no youth is all discreet:
"But sometime stumbles in the course he runs,
"Or shoots one arrow widely from the targe;
"Yet was it not disdain—that seres for ever,—
"Nor was it Hate—that falls forgotten by!
"But all my woe was Youth; and in Youth, Love!
"For know that when our kindly sire the King,
"Went as a pilgrim to the holy Shrine,
"I too, went with him; and as we returned
"We passed this way; and from yon covert there,
"Hearing our voices, duly fearing Man,
"Many a hind leapt out and took the plains.—
"I, being nimble,—enamoured of the chase,
"Tarried awhile, and let our father home.
"So from the shivering dawn till scorching noon
"I hunted: then the fierce sun made me pause
"To reconsider for my home-return;
"And seeking for the track that took the King,
"Afar beneath those trees I chanced to spy
"An old man sitting; hard-by him a maid—
"His merry daughter tending camels there,—
"Like a lithe willow of the garden, tall,
"Excelling Grace!—Wherefore I gave them hail.
"But that old man began to question me
"Of my intent: then I in friendly-wise,—
"'Wilt thou accept a stranger when he comes?'
"He, searching shrewdly, made me a cold salute;

" Muttering: ' Each man even as his means !
" Where-at, like some coy maid, I deftly turned
" To take my steed to water at the pool.
" But he repenting this same churlishness,
" Spake to his child, and she ran willingly
" And brought me milk that waited in the wind ;
" She watered too, my steed: whereby I knew,—
" Oh to what sweet excess !—her loveliness ;
" And all the cool fresh milk of all their herd,—
" Drink that imperious Genii not disdain,
" Thenceforth could quench not the luxuriant thirst
" That burned within me meeting her mere eyes !
" And as I gazed toward her, rooted there
" Myself like some dull stock, her father came
" Bringing me fruit and pasties; saying too,
" ' Bear with the meanness of a poor man's gift !
" ' The Liberal pardon the excuse sincere !'
" So I acccepting hospitality
" In guestly-wise, thereafter made request
" To be a suppliant suitor for his child ;
" Vowing, ' By Him above, who fashioned her
" Beauteous in all her ways beyond excel,—
. " Take all I have,—these jewels,—this my sword,
" My steed, my all, as portion of her dower ;
" And then go forth with me to meet my Tribe ! ' "

" Now all my housings were of gold, inlaid ;—
" Wondrous enwrought by orient labour rare :
" So that old shepherd kindled with amaze
" Regarding them, and with his shrivelled palms
" Blighted the polished jewels, lifting them
" Eagerly up to the light,—then gripped my hands ;
" And, after that, he drove the cattle forth
" Unto his own abode, not far away ;

" And on that night,—O kindly heaven be praised
" For that sweet boon !—I kissed her as my wife ;
" And there was made a lordly feast for us.
" So I abode three days among their tents ;
" And on the fourth day rose to seek my tribe,
" Purposed to bring back all my promised wealth
" And henceforth live with them.   For what to me
" Were all the tribal titles of renown,—
" The petty heritage of hate and fame,
" Against the towered sovereignty of Love ?

 " Now you my brother and my liege, O king,
" Were on a far-off journey when I came ;
" And crownèd not the merry company
" That quaffed my bride and me on that sweet night;
" Yet doubt me not; I was at one with all;
" And on the blithe wings of our general joy
" I sent a trusty slave with gifts of gold ;
" Gems, and sweet manner of remote attires ;
" Moreover camels of the pearliest hair,
" To bring in sort becoming to her rank,—
" (Or liefer to her beauty past all station,
" Being immortal)—my dear wife to me.

 " Days fevered into weeks of maddening doubt
" And trancèd fear, and blank disesperance:
" Till one dark morn, my slave came back to me
" Heavy and worn with anguish and affret,
" O'er-brimming (as you marked) with utter woe ;—
" ' My lord I saw no sign of living soul.
" They were not there.'—And thus, with all my gifts
" Turned every golden one to dull reproach,
" And each of silver to a pledge of grief,—
" I was a gazing-stock—even as a tale
" Fit to be told half-jestingly at large

" By every casual clown,—Incarnate woe !
" Picture me, O my liege lord, me, your brother,
" Lying within their cups of emptied healths,
" More like the laggard worthless lees of wine
" Than like its glory, as erewhile I was !—

" I sent ambassadors to many a tribe
" Using all gentlesse, piled entreaties, bribes,—
" Monies I showered :—but the very coins
" Rang with a mocking sound as from strange hands
" They gathered indolence, got bastard lies,
" Or fruitless honesty.   Ah ! bear with me !
" Judge for me, O my brother, if my Fate
" Heaped not a tragic burden, when it gave
" In such dumb rhetoric such life-long woe !

" I never saw her more !—But for her sake,
" Because of my unsleeping spring of Love,
" I went to be affianced to the Shrine,
" Living in Mecca: and by certain ways
" Came to our native tribe at intervals :—
" But now at this familiar sovenance,
" The flood of ancient sorrow broken aloose,
" Sweeps with a ruthless fury through my soul,
" Till pain unreasons me : but on this spot
" Where now we stand, in scorn of ribald years
" I do renew my unregarded vows ;
" And, O may God lead Her to me at last ! "—

Then Zuhayr, marking not surcease of words,
Stared on the ground in sorrowful amaze,
Harking in memory for what signs of woe
Might rise to testify the tristful tale,
Successless: tho' he honoured him the more.
For Asyed came and went at former times,

Using such words as ease the drooping heart
Even as the leaves that seal the Winter's death ;
And doth it not demand a manlier strength
To gag a shrilling grief, than to contend
With bragging foemen at well-practised arms ?—

    So from his back he took the royal cloak
Purfled all over with fresh-breathing flowers,
And set it on his brother as a sign
Of that fraternal love, seld seen ; albeit
It is the vernal shower to manliness.
Anon came dusky slaves with fleecen scarves
And spread them side by side upon the grass
Under the breathless trees: withal, being noon,
The horsemen forayed, bringing hares and birds,
And speckled bucks and clusters of the date ;
While nimble wine, becooled in sunless cave,
Sparkled out brightly, erst for appetite ;
Thereafter, too, for revelling, riotous ;
So that the thirsty rocks so gaunt and still,
Rang back to every one in sweet proclaim ;—
Disdaining as it were, to stand aloof
For want of guestlier robes.—
                 Then twilight came ;
And 'mid the frailest waft of amber cloud,
Like fruit upon a morning-misted tree,
Above the East the early Pleiads rose ;
But not the bulbul's sugared rivalry
Adown the breezeless vale, nor endless roar
Of battling cataracts thralled the welcome sleep
Nor marred the dreams of Zuhayr and his men.
So there they took sweet ease along the grass.
Now Asyed knelt and prayed amid them there :
At every watch he prayed ; then duteously

Aroused his brother, lest some desert-band
Should take them wareless, sleeping.   But the King
Recked not his warning rede till deafening stoure
With ring of imminent hoofs awoke the vale,
And on them like a storm the robbers swept,
Taking them hurtless, cowed, upon their knees,—
Shackling their hands ; they likewise took the King :
And one alone escaped among the rocks,
And piloted by darkness, found the plain,
Urging to rouse the vengeance of his tribe !
But though in slavish trammels there entoiled,
The King spake calmly, calling one to him,—
" What horsemen are ye ? "—when a youthly knight
Glistening in bossy sheen—as though some star
With all its golden fellows had come down
Upon the evening out of furthest heaven,—
Made answer :—" I am Nazih—sometime chief
" Of all the tribe of Cayan to the South :"—
To him then Zuhayr vehemently rejoined :—
" And dar'st thou, empty Kite, out-wrest the tribe
" Of Abs and Adnan with their prince and King ?—
" By means as sly as furtive jackals use,
" Taking us unalert and full of wine ?—
" Howbe, we weigh misfortune with our gold !"
But Nazih answered, beaming haughtily :—
" Abs and Adnan ! truly Allah be praised !
" Fortune insooth espouses me at last,
" Pitying too much mischance so staunchly borne ;
" I am too glad, ye stars ! "—Then Asyed cried ;—
" Good youth, forbear such words ! what hate have you
" 'Gainst any one of us to use us so,—
" Victims of sour misfortune ? "—

                              Scarce incensed,
Through puffed assurance poised above misprize,
Folding his steely arms, in gentle voice

Nazih replied : "Good Sir, I bear no hate ;
" I owe no grudge nathemore than I owe gifts :
" Yet must I yield ye to the Lord of Lan—
" Obad, son of Temeem, whose child I love,
" And for whose hand I die : for ye alone
" Have foiled me ; and till now my love was vain !
" Have not all told me ?—' Dare not them of Abs !
" Go they not scatheless led by the Lion of lions,—
" ' Antar and his lithe knights ? ' Aye often-times !
" But since the stuff has fallen to my palm,
" I will upraise my palace therewithal,
" And who shall rate me ?—get thee hence, old man ;
" And thank thy reverend silver hairs for life !
" Ever too much of old men I have had !"

So they went forth upon the morning-rise,
Wending the wrinkled waste, a mournful train :—
The Strong embound by servile stratagem ;
(Like Talent hearsed neath tyrant Ignorance,)—
And all the valley-birds forgot to sing.
But ere the Morn had pushed his golden bands
Along the quivering sand a little hour,
A low cloud forced the far blue fronting them,
Spreading enormous pinions like a storm
That shakes its pendent rage along the heaven
Tongueless with terror,—till the general din
Fell to a whispering hush of wonderment ;
For the old Pilot halted ; then shrank back
Beckoning to Nazih : " See, my master, there !"—
And Nazih said : " Nay, some mere coil of sand
Whirling aloft the desert, nothing more !"—
" Nay ! Master, nay ! !—for like a demon vast,
" Throned on calamity, against that cloud
" I see a sable knight ;—mark, my lord, there ! ! !
" Look how his keen spear lightens !—Lo, he comes !—
" Methought he growled out like an angry pard,

" Or was't the muffled mouthing of the storm ?—
" See his dark horsemen : Woe, alack-a·day,
" Misfortune on misfortune, woe on woe !—
" 'Tis Antar !—who shall save us from him now ?—
" O that my white age should behold this day !"—
Thereat another counselled, drawing close ;—
" Do not engage him like your other knights,
" He is like none ! Aye, rather let us turn,
" And save ourselves by flight, than stay and die."—
But Nazih, glowing at the craven words,
Broke on his crest and felled him to the ground,
Shouting : " Away ye cowards ! flee ye sheep !
" And perish where ye may ! but as for me,—
" The crimson breast of Battle shall be fair,
" And Death's lip even as honey to my soul !
" Have I not fought with heroes and with tribes,—
" With lions in their iron fastnesses ?—
" And shall I quail before this braggart knight ?—
" To me the spear is better than reproach,
" And bitter Death more sweet than Life a lie !"
Then all eyes nigh shrank dim beholding them—
Antar son of Shedàd, in all his might,
Tall, like a shape of thunder, cantering on,
Holding a dazzling terror in his hand ;—
Ravining the ground it seemed as he drew near ;—
And Nazih maddening through a storm of sand,
Swift as the whirlwind, to destroy him there
Before them all.—But with his massy shield,
Antar shattered the spear-head ; though the shaft
Glancing aside, laid bare his chafing thigh :
While Abjar, billow-like, rolled man and horse,
Glittering before him on the supple sand
In frolic ruin : swift dismounting there,
Antar took Nazih stunned, and bound him down
Twining a stiff thong round about his limbs ;

And gave him to the keeping of his men.
Then shouted fiercely at his breathless friends,
" Destroy the fleers and release the King."—
So that as fowlers, into one wide net
They took the trembling multitude entire,
Sheafing their nerveless spears.   And Nazih groaned.—
Then Antar did obeisance to his King,
Snatching his skirt to kiss, uprising slow;
While Zuhayr gladly greeting, made request
To be led thenceward home : But Antar said :
" First only, Sire, we bane these craven rats :
" And he must die who squealed their treason on ;
" Else 'twill be said we fear their lean allies ! "—

       So Antar's brother went aloof the throng
Where woeful Nazih pronely lay embound;
But Asyed came persuading him to spare :—
" Is not a living man worth twenty dead ?
" This man from out his own nobility,
" Thro' mercy might be e'en as staunch a friend
" As lately he was valiant as our foe :"—
But heeding not, Shiboob unloosed the thong,
Bent to off-strip the tempting raimenture
Ere he should slay him, till against the sand
The piteous caitive e'en from face to foot
Shone like the morning-star so comely fair,—
Naked but shameless with the perfect man ;
But there around his gentle-turnèd wrist
A glimmering band of curdy chrysoprase
Met in two married images of gold
Fashioned like Lāt and Uzza ; and the sword
Lifted to slay him, turned at Asyed's voice :
For Asyed stooping saw the curious gold
And straightway seized and held it to his lips,

Kissing it passionately till he cried :—
" Whence had you this ! Nay, Heaven !—this hair ! these
    eyes !"
While Nazih, uttering a fervent sigh,
Heavily answered him,—" Since thou alone
" Seemest to pity me, and by thy garb
" And reverent beard, an holier man than these
" Meseems thou must be,—so mere Life allow,
" I tell thee that I am a sireless youth ;
" Nowise one slave-born : and I loved a maid,
" For whose sweet sake I oft have courted Grief,
" Battles and Death : but nathèless unmoved,
" She plays at promises as maidens do ;
" So only to my mother in the world
" Have I confessed my sorrow and my love
" When they oppressed ; howbeit yester-morn,
" Calling me to her, she thus counselled me :—
" ' My son, but one thing hast thou left undone :
" ' And only that fulfilled, can prosper you !
" ' Your lady's father has one airy hope,
" ' And that to him is fairer than the sun,
" ' And sweeter in prospection than his life :—
" ' Which, should your luck transform, all his is yours.
" ' Many a chief has fallen to your sword,—
" ' As if the very land were made of chiefs,
" ' And baser kernes had never a part therein :—
" ' How manifold your captives and your spoils !
" ' How hailed a wonder are you in men's eyes !
" ' Of them how much beloved ! Yet, hark ye, boy :
" ' His chiefest foe rides aweless thro' the land,—
" ' The man before whom every battle reels ;—
" ' Antar, whom men speak of !—Wot you well ?'
" ' Wherefore, away : assail the King of Abs
" ' Who rides to greet his kinsman of the Shrine,
" ' And should to-day await in Teba's vale !

" ' Bring but one Absian captive to his hand,—
" ' The least of Zuhayr's kindred ta'en in arms,
" ' And hath he girls a hundred, they are yours ! '
" I in turn said, ' Mother, Thou sayest well !
" ' Yet have I ever heard men speak of Abs
" ' As if no word could match it,—Tribe of Tribes !
" ' Flinty in battle,—irresistible !
" ' Master of life and death ! ' Then she again ; —
" ' Victory in sooth is God's : yet harbouring fears,
" ' Best you live on a trifler ! Nay, my son,
" ' Rather be worthy and array thyself:
" ' Arm for the fray : and prove this Talisman,
" ' Berylled with Allah's immemorial praise.
" ' Thy father gave it me our bridal-night,
" ' Saying, ' Preserve it ! '—So, an thou succeed,
" ' Worship the God of Zemzen all thy days :—
" ' Like-wise in bondage it may bring release.'—

"I took it: and when I am"—
                                        Asyed then,
Piercing beyond dull mist of timeless doubt,
Fell on his neck and kissed him, weeping loud :—
" My Son ! My Son !—my Dove long-lost is found ! "
And Zuhayr marvelling came and took the lad,
And held his brother's child as 'twere his own,
Kissing him ; then brought Antar there to see ;
When he did likewise, being a gentle knight :
But Nazih trembled, all afraid for joy,
Whelmed with release and love, and eke new life
Stored with delight ; and they returned his shield
And broken spear ; while Antar took a robe
Woven of gold, befringed with eagle-plumes,—
And asking freedom, clasped it round his prince
As he would say " I readier give than take :
" Be this a covenant betwixt us twain ! "

Then they began to journey to their tribe :
Zuhayr and Antar first ; Prince Asyed next
Beside his son :—these-after, prisoners came
Closed with an Absian guard, and motley spoils :
And ere the sun had left the level sand
They sat rejoicing in the Absian tents.

    Erelong the King did give a banquet there ;
And Selima and Dhimeya came thereto :
So that the mystery, in one royal flame
Of Joy and Love was tried ; and Love was king !
So Asyed stayed among them till he died,
When Zuhayr laid him softly to his rest
Aneath the Tamarisk, even in Teba's Vale !

1880.

HOW ANTAR FOUND THE SWORD DHAMI!

Now ANTAR rode along the radiant hills
Three days, and met no foe, and heard no sound
Save Abjar's hoofs upon the crisping sand,
From morn till noon ; from noon till with the breeze
Wafting the musk-rose and the song of birds,
Drew from the craggier vallies echoing loud
The growl of mouthing lions, fitfully
Quivering the air.   But when the fervent sun
Uprising lit again the peakèd hills
And glanced on ebon Abjar 'neath his Lord,
Antar, to keep aloof the dazzling flames,
Turned through an opening where two great hills met
Making a mazy vale for tumbling streams
Amidst embowering woodland : then with joy
For sweetness of the air and soothing shade,
He passed on slowly, listening to the streams.
    When as some leopard breathless from his lair
Athwart the twilight spies two antelopes
Locked in encounter, yet of them unseen
For screen of leaves or rocks enshrouding him,
With politic feet makes pause for more delight,
Playing with appetite,—so Abjar paused—
Pricking his nimble ears : for thro' the song
The falling streams enwove, he knew the ring
Of meeting shields and din of griding blades ;

So sifted battle from the loud concent,
Making a still eclipse along the path
Upon the early grass ; yet, noting not,
The chieftain only heard the valley-streams,
Till leaning forward o'er his saddle-bow,
Hard-by, like angry levin through the leaves,
Upleapt a blazing sword in act to strike.
There-after rose the sudden whirr of steeds,
He shouting on the fighters : "Stay your hands !
"Sons of Arabia, let me know your cause ! "
When seeing him, the younger of two knights
Starting aside addressed him reverently :—
" Valorous Antar, warrior-lion of lions,—
" Eagle of armies, ruler of victories,
" To thee, O Prince, I gladly urge my cause ;
" For thou wilt save it seeing it so wronged ! "
ANTAR answered him :—"Lad, that too will I
" With knightly pledge an thou dost name it me,
" And wherefore ye twain slay each other here,
" Alone among the mountains, far from men."
Angrily then the elder turning aloof,
Flouted the timeless counsel and growled there,
Gnawing his lip between ill-mutterings :
While he the fairer, standing crimson-starred
In splintered armour, this-wise made rejoin :—
" Know then, thou noblest knight of all the age,
" We are two brothers, children of one Sire—
" Amru the son of Harith, Teba's son.—
" Whilom as Teba rested in the plain,
" Sleep overtook him, and his camels strayed ;
" He meanwhile dreaming that the goodliest
" Wandering apart was that day lost to him ;
" And waking there-upon, bestirred the herds,
" From whom one answered him :—' O know, my Lord,
" ' Yestreen that gentle camel brake astray.

" ' I followed her and played her till the night
" ' Around the sandy hillocks, one by one,
" ' Till from sheer weariness at all her tricks,
" ' Her sleek hair silvering on the rising dusk,
" ' I spread my hand upon a glittering stone
" ' That lay like some fair star upon the sand,
" ' Which hurlen hard, so smote upon the beast
" ' Piercing her tender neck,--it issued out,
" ' Letting her life sweep darkly o'er the sand.
" ' Thereto approached, I found the camel dead ;
" ' While crimsoned close beside her in the gore,
" ' Lay the weird stone.'—Which, when my great-sire heard, '
" Sorrowing he bade that shepherd lead him forth
" To see the camel lying and the stone ;
" But when he came thereat and saw the stone,
" Found it a thunderbolt ; so bare it home,
" And gave it to a smith from Samarcand
" That from it he might fashion him a sword
" Mighty and glorious,—aye, past every sword !

" Now when betimes the cunning smith returned
" Bringing the Glory, TEBA took it pleased,—
" Deeming its beauty but a faithful glass
" Wherein the Virtues round his Valour shone,
" And pleasantly besought the fashioner :—
" ' What name, Sir Smith, hath this child at your hand ?
" But scoffingly the lusty wight laughed-out :—
" ' Dhami, this brand is hight, O son of Ghalib :
" ' For it is keener than the scythe of Death ;
" ' But where's the warrior who can smite with it ?'—
" There-with my great-sire gripped it in his hand,
" ' Roaring :—' For him,—the smiter,—I am He !'
" And at one stroke clave down the curly head,
" And the dumb trunk fell weltering to the ground.
" So through the world there is no sword like that.

" A sheath of gold thereafter he enwrought,
" And kept it in his treasure-house till death.
" My father too, in such-wise held the sword,
" Till life nigh-gone, he bade them send to me ;
" And when I kneeled beside his bed, quoth he :—
" ' My son, thy brother was a tyrant born,
" ' Lusting for violence and from Truth divorced ;
" ' Loveless toward all men, and by all unloved :
" ' Among all women deems himself beloved :—
" ' Among his kind—hath never known a friend !
" ' And well wot I, he will usurp thy right.
" ' Wherefore take now the Dhami : hide it fast :
" ' Let none behold it, nor thee hiding it :
" ' But when thy brother shall fore-seize thy share,
" ' Do thou, my son, content thee with the sword :
" ' For if thou give it to the King of Kings,—
" ' Chosroe, lord of lords,—the glorious one,—
" ' He will enrich thee, and thy lot is fair ;
" ' Patience indeed, will prove your best of friends :
" ' For though sore-taxed by small things, oft enslaved,
" ' A man by Patience is the lord of all.'
" Straightway I went, and from the treasure-house
" Took forth the gorgeous Dhami glittering keen,
" Like some strange meteor that out-lustres day,—
" And the slow dawn out-winging, hid it here,
" In one of these small silver dunes, perdiè.
" And even on the morn my sire lay dead,
" My brother greedily engrossed his wealth,
" Sparing me naught, nor even recking right ;
" Yet when he sought the Sword and found it not,
" Raved like a storm upon me : so I told
" That ere the dawn-rise I had hidden it here ;
" Wherefore, most noble Prince, we lately came
" In search thereof ; natheless we found it not :
" And he, berating me from place to place,

" Vainly fingering every spot of sand,
" Leapt like a maniac at me, crying aloud :—
" ' Villain thou mock'st me, knowing well where it lies.'—
" So till Thou cam'st barely I hoped escape,
" Breaking his blows."
                    And Antar pitied him,
Seeing him beautiful and soft of soul ;
Withal a perfect knight in his demean.
But turning sharplier where the elder stood,
Haughtily cried out on his tyrantship :
" He who so ill regards a dead man's wish,
" Little, I ween, respects the living man !
" Yet, for it is not good to use men thus,
" Living or dead,—take gentleness to you :
" Civil to men for mankind man should be :
" For manners, like the floats that fishers use
" To buoy their lines, do mark the rights of man,
" And keep the general honour of the race.
" This is your father's son,—should share his love,
" Finding your tongue of all men's least a sword,—
" Finding your arm of all arms least a foe's ;
" And so, of all hearts, your heart most his friend."

    But he enangered at the indignant words,
And deeming Antar but a braggart-knight,—
Nowise his equal (for his face was dark
Resembling the complexion of the slaves :)—
Foamed on him like some wild-ox, random-wise,
Challenging deeds.   So Antar left no field
Either to rein or wheel, ere his true lance
Smote thro' the chest ten spans and hurled him dead,
Clean from the quivering steed along the ground ;—
Then called the youth, and spake to him such words :—
" Go to your father's house : assume his rank ;
" Henceforth if any tyrant thralls your path,
" Send and apprize me, and his life is yours."

Sc the lad raised a chain from off his neck,
Golden and precious, which his mother wore
Dying in Hima,—and to Antar gave :
(And this was Amru, who became his friend.)
Then passing forth, beheld the late-slain man,
Saying :—" Now he is gone, I have no foe."
And so went home ; while Antar fixed his spear :
And tethering Abjar, rested him awhile
To muse upon the story of those twain :
And as he played his fingers in the sand
Where the thin drift swelled whitelier through the grass,—
Lifted a stone, and under it beheld,
E'en like a rainbow chiding the dull clouds,—
The jewelled haft ; so drew the wonder forth,
Shaking the moist sand from it till it shone
Like to the iterant lightning, dazzlingly,—
Sword of all swords,—the only sword of all !—
Then ANTAR knew that Allah prospered him,
And passed along the valley by the streams.

ANTAR RETURNING FROM PERSIA.

MOTIVE: *Antar coming from Persia discovers Abla captive; rescues her, and recounts his adventures.*

EVEN as a tristful dove in April-tide,
Bereft its mate—bemocked of amorous winds,
Mourns at the cheerful noon-day, and at night
Fitfully flutters through the dreaming leaves,—
So Abla, captive in the robbers' camp,
Standing a Queen of Grief amid her maids
Moaned to the evening, pining for dim Death.
Now Antar coming from the King of Kings,
Leading much treasure to his father's land,
Passing Azool on Abjar in the dusk—
Heard the desolate harp-string, and he sighed,—
"O for Thy voice, for Thy songs, O my Love!"
And ere the whisper slept upon his lips,
Startling the trancèd air arose a dirge,
Wafting his soul's wings through those olden days
What-time by shimmering pools, in Shurebàh
The bulbul sang of Abla; while himself,
Along the garden watched the giddying stars
Dive in the ripples of the lotus-flowers,
And moths that mooned around Syringa-trees!
So there he reined to list the plaintive strain,
　　"Weep for our glory: Weep for our hero: Weep abun-
　　　　dantly!
　　　O my eyes unceasingly pour ye fountains of sorrow!
Antar is dead ; my warrior, prostrate ; slain exultantly :—
　　　　(*Chorus*) Fallen, fallen!

" He was the vigilant sword of our honour, drawn forth
    valiantly ;
  Where he lightened even the warriors shouted for
    succour.
  Where is thy strength my knight? and thy heart that
    loved amazingly ?—
        (*Chorus*) Stricken with shadows !
" Weep for your Hero, Absians, here in dire captivity ;
  Dash your hands, ye beautiful ones, on desolate faces :
  Grieve must we, aye and for ever, mourning our prince
    illustrious.
        (*Chorus*) Valorous Antar !"
·Till with his name it died upon the breeze.
But Antar wondering, eased the burning reins,
And straining low beheld the child of Malik—·
She, the dove of the tamarisk—his life :—
She,—the musk-rose of the night—his Love,—
Dark with dishevelled ringlets, weeping there,
Captive Beauty of Beauties : so he turned,
Musing a moment an' it were no dream ?
Then, marking where the slaves that kept her stood,
Blazed as a flame at them, and slew them ; so
That two alone escaped across the night,
Gasping in helpless terror as they fled :—
" Antar still lives !—Hide us thou dust ! alas !"—
But Abla knew him ; though she stood for tears,
Like one who whitely peers upon the Spring,
Loosely raimented : her veil upraised :
Tranced with the tender vision of new life,—
(Seeing Shiboob had rumoured Antar's death,
Knowing him fallen in the battle-pool) ;
Howbeit on the plumes of Night he came
Bringing her Life and Freedom and true Love !
Then, with one sweet small cry of utter joy,
E'en as a doveling erst among the leaves,

Fell to his folding arms that strongly closed
Around her breathless bosom, clasping her
Even as a dark Cloud clips the little Moon
Sinking toward mount Sadi in the Spring ;
Or as a blithe stream clips a willowy isle,
Singing weariless :—so he held his Love,
Kissing her mute lips till new roses came
And the fresh tears re-bloomed the olden smile.
Then Abla's maiden fetched a golden bowl,
Dainty, abrim with juice of Indian grape,
Fragrant of south flowers or of luscious airs
That wander in the vallies of Cashmère :
And Abla kissed the bowl before he drank,—-
Anon began to shew him all that passed
After her father Malik urged him forth
(Plotting his death) to gain a hapless dower,—
The thousand matchless camels of the king :
And how Shiboob, believing Antar dead,
Hurried the fatal rumour to her tribe,
Cursing her father Malik for the deed.
In turn, then, Antar, answered smilingly,
" Yea, they were thousands ; and we were but two :—
" But Love is more envalouring than hosts !
" So we fought on and slew them, even as leaves
" When the red-handed Autumn storms along,
" Baring the tristful trunks,—aye, flourished, too,
" Till Abjar stumbled, when they bound me fast,
" And haled me to the presence of the King.
" Now Munzir asked me gently whence I came,—
" Whether a warrior of my tribe, or slave ?—
" And I obedient, answered in this-wise :
" ' Among all liberal ones, O king renowned,
" ' The skilful sword-cut and the spear-thrust keen,
" ' With patience in the blinding battle-dust,
" ' Pleads with the noble-souled.   The tribe of Abs

" ' Owns me its champion in the storm of war :
" ' Aye, in the moment when the fiery trump
" ' Welds faithful hearts to one triumphant sword,
" ' I am a star before it, leading on.
" ' Yestreen, O king, I slew the prince of Tai,—
" ' Rebeeah, and King Zuhayr sang my deed ;
" ' But Malik, envious, (for I love his child),
" ' Weeting to make my death, devised for me
" ' To win new dowry for my bride—to-whit,—
" ' A thousand camels of my liege, the King's :
" ' Love is my fate ; and failing Love, I die.
" ' Therefore, I chose what most like Death meseemed,
" ' Or still more glorious Life in perfect Love,
" ' And here, O King, I stand before my Doom ! '—
" Munzir, the king, sat smiling : then peered round
" On all his wise ones, till anew he asked :
" ' Why for mere Love, I perilled all my life ?—
" ' Why for a desert-flower, I risked my All ?'—
" I replied him : ' Love is the Lord of Death.
" ' Under Arabian veils, the eye of Love
" ' Hurling his lightnings, is than Death himself
" ' A thousand-thousand-fold more perilous :
" ' Yea, keener than revengeful scimetars !—
" ' Even the bravest bow before his might,
" ' Encountered wareless by the Fire of fires.—
" ' May God give Malik the dark cup of Death
" ' At this my hand for his obsequious art,—
" ' Urging me onward to insidious Death !
" ' Did not a Maiden weep when I went forth ?—
" ' Sweetly I think she cries my not-return !
" ' O to the bright wild places where she dwells,
" ' Enwaft ye Lightnings my last breath of Love :
" ' Wait in vain ye Absian steeds for me
" ' To fly, Death's angel, o'er your crimson fields !
" ' Ye that love the groves of tamarisk-trees,

" ' Mourn at the raven—the keen evening-wolf!
" ' Moan at the wandering leopards of the night !
" ' Woe to your warrior sorrowing in gyves,—
" ' Held fast by jangling fetters ! '
       Then the king
" Praised the poor words, and all the court around
" Murmured for mercy. Sudden a mortal cry,
" Mingled with wail of women from without,
" Bade e'en the king's guard leave me, rushing forth ;
" And lo, a great lion breaking from his cage
" Had leapt upon a kinsman of the king,
" And made the flying people sick with fear !
" Wherefore I begged them straightway take me forth
" To let me slay him, and so save the man. ·
" Then, being ungyved, with this same sword I went,
" And in the open, calling thy sweet name,
" Shore through the thunderous face atween the eyes,
" And left the tawny glory,—like a cloud
" Encrimsoned in the falling of the sun :—
" And all the city came to see him dead.

" Now Munzir, vassal to the King of Kings—
" Chosroe, Lord of the East, the mighty Prince,—
" Drew home, enangered from his Master's court.
" For at a goodly feast the Monarch held,
" Before each guest a dish of dates were set,—
" An almond in each date instead the stone :
" But in king Munzir's date they left the stone.
" So when he marked his Liege and all the court
" Eat of the fruit and make no more ado,
" He like-wise, mid their tittering, left no stone,—
" Weeting no jest until he left the land !
" Then urging homeward, full of vague revenge,
" He, worrying all the border, shed much blood.
" Then Chosroe sent his chivalry elect

" To bring him bound a prisoner; and the fight
" Fell sore for Munzir till dividing Night
" Severed the battlers, and they drew me forth
" Ridding the chains to speak before the king;
" When hearing the repulse, to him quoth I:
" ' Behold, O king, a plealess enemy,
" ' Alone,—a captive!—yet, return my arms!
" ' Give me my sword, my shield,—my ebon steed,—
" ' An hundred horsemen to defend my rear,—
" ' And I will be as Winter to your foes.
" ' Then, if I win, assign me sole reward
" ' That hapless dowry—all the thousand beasts!'
" So Munzir smiled and made an holy oath.

" Forthwith, at sunrise, vowing by thine eyes,
" That are my soul, my strength, my arms, my All,
" I, Antar, thirsting as parched Earth for rain,
" Took the first Persian horde and swept it down—
" As men mow down the grass on summer plains;
" So that its ruin shimmered in the night;
" And afterward I sent my challenge forth
" To Khosrevàn, that we, the leaders twain,
" Meeting together, so might end the war!—

" So from his serried ocean, on the morn,
" Like to a blazing sun, he issued forth,
" Waving a brand of fire; and on his head
" He wore a golden morion, diamonded
" With stones of Hindi, mystic, glittering;
" And in four leathern loops at saddle-bow
" Were four small darts,—each one a feathered flame
" While proudly under him a glorious steed,
" Flecked on its forefront with a crescent moon,
" Drew to the fight.—
                        " As when some giant rock

" Hurls a huge billow back along the main
" Sheer at the next still mightier till in foam
" Of glorious minglement their lines are lost,—
" So in two rolling shocks of sand we met,
" And neither army saw us till the breeze
" Let through the fluctuant haze his fiery helm,
" And I once more espied the fairy moon
" Empearled upon the fore-head of his steed.—
" Anon I reft him of his beamy lance,
" Bidding him draw his axe ; but crazed for rage,
" He sported like some young lion with his dam,
" Till wearying that, he snatched a glittering dart
" In hope to spoil the glory of my steed ;
" But it flew off my targe like some swift bird
" When one opposes him in full flight home ;
" And all those kindred-perils followed it,
" Bringing my vantage, when I thy name sang,—
" Flinging my nimble mace like some slung stone ;
" But he, well-weeting that it winged his doom,
" Uttered a cry, and strained his bright shield round
" Between his shoulders where the terror crashed
" Clean through the shield, and snapped him like a branch.
" Then all his men for rage brought back the fight,
" So that the great plain groaned unceasingly
" Under the tumult, like a wintry strait
" Where-on the proud ship lives by chance alone.
" But in their wrath,—their Captain lying lost,—
" Fortune unveiled them but a marbled Woe :
" For Munzir drave them toward a raging stream,
" And thrust them head-long from his wrangling blades,
" Utterly overborne as in some fire
" Where drossy ores are whelmed !
                              " Now in the court,
" Zamir, the loved adviser of the king,
" Keener for Peace than War, befriended me.

" But Chosroe's sour defeat being noised afar,
" Zamir set out unknown to Persia's court,—
" Wishing to glean how men received it there ;
" Tho', there-arrived, heard no man speak thereof ;
" Yet found the town aflutter with one name—
" ' Dread Badramoot'—a peerless christian knight,
" Defender of the Grecian Argosy
" That brought the golden tribute of the isles
" Across opposing seas, by many a strait ;
" Which tribute, he, on challenge, now denied
" Till beaten singly by a mightier knight;—
" And there-withal, ten nobles of the court
" Fell in ten days beneath his cruel brand—
" And gentle Chosroe wept upon his throne,
" In dread to lose the Lordship of the Isles !
" Then, as a sunny vision, Zamir's voice
" Came in upon his anguish: ' Hear, O king ;
" ' Quaff not too deeply of this cup of Woe.—
" ' Though grief gives kings their highest dignity,—
" ' And grief itself is royal, and can raise
" ' The beggar to the level of a king :—
" ' Yet, cherished to excess, it is a vice
" ' Which turns the beggar to a crazy fool,
" ' And puts fantastic rags on Majesty.—
" ' See: at proud Munzir's court, in durance still,
" ' Is valiant Antar, even he who spoiled
" ' Your army, yea, assailed and slew their Chief,—
" ' Leaving his body to the hungry Night.
" ' Grant him a royal permit: give him smiles;
" ' And if it be the will of frolic Fate,
" ' I doubt not he shall slay this vaunter, too.'
" Wherefore they brought me to the King of Kings,
" Courting encounter with this Badramoot ;
" But when I viewed the splendour of the King,
" And saw his face embrighten, like a cloud

" Of rain that passes from against the sun,
" I knelt down there before his ivory throne,
" And sang before him and his listening lords.
" Then spake king Chosroe smiling graciously;—
" To-night, O Warrior, shall this starry robe
" ' Glory around thee if thou slay that man.'—
" But Badramoot stood bantering at my song,
" Towering among his silken worshippers ;
" Anon did grasp me gently by the hand
" As he should say 'Nay, keep your life: forbear !'
" Till, thro' a myriad glimmering scimitars,
" A Herald led us from the whispering throng
" Out to the golden gate before the plain,—
" Where Abjar neighed beside the marble stair,
" Eager for battle.   But in that same hour
" The blustering braggart fell down overcome ;
" For Dhami smote him sheer upon the crown,
" And played down grievously between his arms;—
" (E'en as the fiery levin smiting the crest
" Of some tall oak may cleave it down the trunk:)—
" So that the people stared agape for joy, —
" Then hurried me once more before the king.
" Thus on that eve I wore the glorious robe ;
" And at the banquet that the great king made,
" He gave an hundred Nobles for my train,
" And silken Tunics jewelled like the night,
" With treasure limitless.
                              " Then Munzir came
" Entreating peace with Chosroe, bringing there
" The thousand Camels for the promised dower,
" And there withal this moonbeam of a spear
" Wherewith I slew these slaves ! But in the night,
" Lonely beside my couch, I wept and sang :—
            " ' O sullen day, O churlish night,
                Twin tyrants to my heart ye are

Ye care not if a brow be bright ?—
　Nor reck ye if a form is fair ?—
Blaze out thy light, O Day !
　Burn out thy stars, thou Night ;
Your pageants old bemock with play,
　My heaven-o'erwearied sight !

" ' As twilight hides our golden day,
　Dim distance veils my Abla's face ;
Light, Night and Space, my spirit slay ;
　Gross Darkness fills her place.
Yet bright and dark are now the same ;
　For day and night are one
To those whose hearts' immortal flame
　Outreigns the envious sun !

　O hallowing light of Love !
　" ' Thou fragrant-embered fire
　　O phœnix of Desire !
　O heavenly-tender dove !
　The gardens of the soul
　　Thy voice enfills will spring ;
　　The rivers as they sing
　Give not so sweet a dole !
　My life puts forth her leaves ;
　　My heart her rose renews ;
　　Passion my soul endues,
　That crownless grieves :—

　" ' Our eyes meet not: we yearn !
　　Lips kiss that may not touch :
　　We that love over-much
　Thus inly burn
　Our separate fires of Love
　　On Earth,—whose fadeless claim
　　Will make our single flame
　In Heaven above.'

" Yet lest I weary thee with deed on deeds
" Lily of maidens, let me lastly tell
" How on a morning ere I left the realm,
" Munzir, and Mubidan, the High-Priest, came
" And led me to a fane of blazing brass—
" Candied with all imaginable gems,
" Wonder of every age—the Shrine of Fire,—
" Wherein I saw lithe flames of aloe-wood
" Hovering fragrant like a dewy veil,
" Gleaming tremulous,—while sweet Magian words
" Turned to the music of a thousand strings
" And devious voices, filled the mystic hall,
" Pouring a shadowed summer, as it were,
" Thro' all the fluttering dreamland of my soul !
" For here a vision of thy beauty, Sweet,
" Floated before me on the quivering air ;
" And in the flame I saw thee leaning-wise,
" Under a palm-tree by Euphrates' side,
" Musing mournfully on the bright wide stream—
" The Houri of the hill-flowers kissing thee,
" Holding a broken dart within its hand ;
" And all the stars fled weeping thro' the sky !
" Yet this was but the fancy of the flames ?
" Lo! here I sit beside thee at Azool,
" From all my quest enfortuned in the end ;
" And on the near horizon neath yon star
" Myriads of camels bring their loads of silk,
" Sabean spices, and a diadem
" (Which Chosroe gave me for our bridal-day)
" Enleaved with emerald and enflowered with pearl,
" Topped with an opal moon."

          While yet he spake,
Abjar, the steed, drew near them; and he turned
From her white arms and looked along the dusk,
Where a strange band of horsemen stirred the sand,—

And knew the thieves had come to slay him there.
But hearkening not the little cry she made,
Like to a furrowing fire of lightning, flashed
Clean in their midst, and wheeling, slew them there,
Uttering a cry : and some few fled like birds,—
Thinking a desert-demon followed them.

Prinking the sand anon, Canopus, high,
Brought on the labouring train to soft Azool ;
So there the tent of Love was pitched that night.

Hadífah, son of Zalim, made a feast
For all the Chieftains of Fazarah's tribe ;
And Kervash, cousin to the King of Abs,
Káis, the son of Zuhayr,—came thereto.

What-time the massy beakers glittered round,
Battles and heroes blazed from tongue to tongue
With friendly alternation, each to each,
Till one guest tiring of the tedious praise
Of Human-kind, upheld his brimming cup,
And quaffed its glory to the headlong steed,—
' That groanless wades the fiery battle-flood,
' Nerving his lord to spurn at Death himself
' And all the eager tumult of keen spears.'—
But Kervash answered from the hushed applause ;—
" Soothly we do right well to laud the Steed ;
" Yet praising it past Woman is excess ;
" Though I have known it loved more lavishly.
" Albeit there is no other steed but One :—
" Beyond compare the heaven-best horse of all :
" And that is Dahis; and the king of Abs,
" Káis my cousin,—tends it with his hands,
" Disdainless: for Love makes the unclean clean."
And thus-much praised it till his host arose,
And turning said, " O Kervash, err no more ;
" The Speech was unadvised; for all men know

" That this land owns no horses like to ours !
" Fleeter than eagles they outrival all.
" Now let a slave bring forth the goodliest here,
" That we may bid our guest re-shape his words,
" And pay due tribute to the steed of steeds :
" How-be, mark that one : "—For a slave drew nigh,
Leading a courser, lean-flanked, beautiful,—
And the pavilion whispered willow-wise,
Till Hamil said to Kervash, " Gentle friend,
" Boldly admit—and therein earn our praise,—
" Your king's horse is no match for this of ours ! "
But Kervash smiling, peered along the beast ;
Then switching flippantly, made gay response :—
" The fodder of the King's horse for one day
" Would purchase this: though your beast does you praise!"
Whereat, they brought the pride of all the stalls,—
Ghabra, the nimble mare, broad-chested, tall,
Hard-hoofed and open-nostrilled, like the wind
In lightness : and her tail swept on the ground
Making a silken sound, like hidden brooks
That sing among the shingle toward the sea.
Hadifah then went close and spake to her ;
And by her jewelled tether led her on
Till she stood pawing, winning much regard :
For no man spake a word ; but held his peace
Looking at Kervash first, then on the steed
Glowing in beauty, sweet in all her ways.
Forthwith he cried aloud: " Now look at her ;
" And like a prince among assembled chiefs,
" Avow you never yet beheld her peer ! "
Kervash (silent for awhile) exclaimed,
" The dew that sparkles in the golden pails
" Wherewith the Dahis doth assuage his thirst,
" Would far out-price this vaunted steed of yours :
" But nathëless, is this a worthy steed."

Then Hamil glowing with dissembled wrath,
Shouted :—" Not even our Ghabra ? "—and remained
Anear his hrother, rooted, full of scorn.
Again spake Kervash :—" Nay, nor any steed
" That heretofore hath pleased the eye of Man !
" This Dahis you misdeem I overpraise,
" Would trick the swiftest coursers of your tribe— ·
" Weighted with many quintal-loads, to-boot ! "
Then they twain brightening at the queer conceit,
Opened a bargain that on such a day,
Dahis and Ghabra out before the tribes
Should start abreast on an elected course :—
Withal, the master of the victor-steed
Should from his rival take as many beasts—
He or she-camels, as would give him meed.
But Kervash seeing craft in carelessness,
Asked that the king, being loser, should repay
Twenty she-camels of the pearliest hair.
And thus the balmy evening took them there ;
While Aldebàran shot his fiery beams
Over the silver-coronetted hills,
Rising afar serenely.
                            But with morn
Kervash arose and went to them of Abs,
Out to the dayset, and bespoke the king ;
And blithely told him of the compromise.
Then Káis rose in silence chidingly,
Striding along his bright pavilion, fierce,
And petulantly breaking forth at him :
" Kervash, it is not good that thou hast done,—
" Compacting thus with men unknown to thee !
" A man may hold his place as honoured guest
" And keep him for himself responsible,
" Being familiar with all sweet discreetness ;
" But rashly thus to implicate his friend,

" Is indiscriminate folly, and must sour
" Past all re-cure our gentle cup of Love.
" You might have chaffered, aye, with all the World,
" And in the sum-result, it were more safe
" Than to have staked a yeanling with this man !
" For he is full of pretext,—ugly shifts ; ·
" Will rub the tenderest law: but never graze it !—
" Kindly with sound advice; in judgment, rare !
" But with his purse—a tyrant, save what-time
" The sails of reputation suffer storm:
" When he would piece them from his sailor's backs ;
" And iron turns to wool upon his tongue :—
" Moreover had my brother done this thing,
" Still had my blame gone hard with Him: but you,—
" You but my uncle's son—it is too much ! "

Then Kervash grew afraid, perceiving him
Thus hurt at his un-wisdom ; so went forth,
Lifting aside the curtain of the tent,
Smiting his breast.
               But Káis got to horse,
And rode alone away until he stood
Even at the open door of Hamil's tent,
And found the brothers feasting there-within ;
Whereat they rose, and greeting, drew him in.
He being en-hungered nathéless, spake not,
But like a generous chieftain, bared his arms,
And banqueted so bravely that they stared ;
While humouring his jovial-hearted-ness,
Hadifah thus began : " In most affairs
" Our cousin Káis does right royally :
" But royallest of all in appetite."—
Therewith King Káis peering at them both,
Answered :—" In sooth good cousins, I do well :
" Yet not to eat your pasties am I here ;

" Neither to rape your virgin wines withal :
" But to unfile this fetter Kervash locked !
" Since 'tis a law among the Chivalrous,—
" A wager bears not that the tankard breeds !
" Wherefore I pray you, let it be unyoked ! "
Hadîfah, deftly patient, made reply,—
" The argument is old. The wager, new.
" The last is sovereign to my reverence :
" I cannot quit the bet till in my stalls
" These twenty plighted camels take their food.
" Thereafter will I mention it no more.
" Albeit if it rather please the king
" That I should take them, or by grace renounce,
" Our kith shall witness; and his will is done ! "
So they twain tossed the stake this way and that;
And Hamil smiled to see the crimson glow
Flower-like o'erspread the king's face as he rose
And (torn with reckless anger), cried aloud,
" How could my kinsman bet with such as ye ?
" What was his pledge ? "—Then Hamil overjoyed,
Seeing the king's wrath waxing unadvised,
Lightly returned. " She-camels twenty, Sire ! "
Then Káis, urged on by the nimble wine,
Cried: " 'Tis a pauper's wager; be it void,—
" Or be it thirty ! "—and rejoining swift,
Hadîfah shouted " forty ! "—Thus it leapt
'Twixt careless Pride and Cunning, till it stood :—
" An hundred camels of the pearliest hair ! "—
So Káis signed the compact ; while around,
A press of old and young came gathering,
Mooning amaze to hearken to their terms.
Then Hamil urged the limit of the race ?—
Whereat the king said : " Forty arrow-flights !
" And there is Ayas, child of wide renown,
" The errless archer—who shall mete it out.

" Therefore appoint ye when the Day shall be ! "
Then Hamil, for the training of the steeds,
Bid for each several arrow-flight a day :
Moreover, that the level by the lake
Zatu'l-Irsàd would well befit the race.
So Káis plighted all, and went his way.
But when the king had passed from out the throng
Ayas the archer strode to Hamil's side,
And frowning sharply at the brothers twain,
Forth-spake: "O fools, what is it ye have done ?—
" Hereby one sees how Craft with Wisdom foins ;
" Their King is stainless; but your churlishness,—
" Your doggish greed forlays some trap for him,
" Which, though 'tis meant for one man's petty gain,
" Will utterly inflame two friendly states
" With such an hungry and tempestuous fire
" The blood of generations may not quench.
" O think upon it!   Ponder well for us !
" Withal, the dainty Dahis is a steed
" Whose hoofs are fire-brands in the night of battle ;—
" Yea, as the lightning of a hurricane ;
" And with their music make the rocks resound ;
" Aye, there is none in all the land his like !

        Hadifah, humming softly, then replied:
" O Ayas, think not we shall veer our course !
" Abuse in anger gains mere rhetoric ;
" But loses true appeal : so use it not.
" We shall not shrink : all things will choose their parts.
" While we must act the husband of Occasion.
" Howbeit, I love the camels of the King.
" It was a simple bargain ;—nothing more ;
" The person of a king can nothing change it,
" With all the harness of his royalty !
" Ours is a merry bet ;—no policy ! "

But Ayas swaiped aside among the crowd,
Aflush with hate and burning discontent:
And many murmured at him : for, said they,
" Hamil at least doth surely mean us well !
" Have we not been too quiet in the camp,—
" Fray-less, inactive :—and this new emprise,—
" A famous race,—will bring good cheer to all?
" But whatsoever hap, the thing is good."—

So Káis trained his horse for forty days :
Encouraging his graces with sweet toil ;
So that his fire and strength and beauty grew
Matchlessly intermarried, perfect-wise :
And when the full moon shone the second time,
Unto the lonely level by the lake
The Absian horsemen thronged, and all the tribe
Of Adnan and the Fazarean tribe.

Then Ayas turned his back upon the lake,
And veering northward, shot his quiver forth
Before them following, till he made an end,
And all the forty barbs were held again.
The while they halted, from between two clouds,
A shaft of golden light, swift-travelling,
Sparkled, as on a topaz, in the south,
Athwart some wonder hailing from afar
Like an attirèd pursuivant of heaven.
And all stood mute, astonied, as it came ;
Till as it drifted near, the jealous beam
Seemed to be sporting—even like a bird,
That lures the cunning searcher from its nest,
Now wheeling round it and now flown aside :—
Until a universal shout arose :—
" 'Tis Antar !"—and forthwith made visible,
Like Night when some rare comet spans her arch,
Abjar the sable Glory of the plains

Brought on the hero, and men soon beheld
The fatal Dhami glittering at his side,—
Its haft all-sugared-o'er with flower-like gems ;—
Like Winter hiding in the shade of Spring !—
So Antar's brother went afoot to him
With the king's greeting, and they twain drew on
Right to the middle of the motley throng
Till Antar stood obeisant by the King ;
While Hadifah atremble, saw him close,
Standing among his friends ; but ANTAR said,—
Keenly espying him :—" Illustrious Ones,
" I heard the bruit of this race afar ;
" For our belovèd king has sanctioned it !
" Therefore, what more is left but that the steeds
" Be loosed? The Victory is God's alone,—
" The peerless God of all the day and night ;—
" The King of life, whose chamberlain is death ;
" By whose fair Shrine, I swear, and by the fount
" Of Zemzem's crystal everflowing stream,—
" If Hadifah by craft or otherwise,
" Winning or losing, doth oppress or vex,
" The cup of Death and vengeance be his pain !—
" For all the glory of his tribe shall be
" Even as a fable told.   O Absian chiefs,
" If that this race must be, then be it just !
" Or by the eyes of Abla, this my steed
" Shall dye his ebon fetlocks red with gore
" Plunging among the slain."   And all aloud .
In fierce acclaim, cried : " Antar, He is right ! "

Then Káis becked the jockey to his side,
Counselling gently :—" Give not all the rein :
" If any moisture dews upon his flank,
" Stroke your limb o'er it lightly, wiping it ;
" Press not albeit more than feather's-weight
" Along his loins, lest he may prove distressed."—

Hadifah heard him; straightway his bespoke
Even in such-wise,—uttering those same words,—
Teaching to tend his mare: and Antar laughed,
Then scornfully cried out:—" O this mimic fool,
" Who sticks his dead Conceit with borrowed plumes,
" Yearning to counterfeit true Royalty,
" And snatch deceived attention from the nonce!—
" Howbeit, our noble tongue is not so poor,—
" So inly starved,—with tattered rags misclad,
" That one should need to steal such sovereign phrase!
" Princes alas, in all their least effects
" Must models be for Ignorance the ape;
" But I, for one, say that from following him
" In merest words, your jade will follow his!"—

Hadifah passed on like a sulky cloud,
Growling:—" My own horse shall not run to-day!"
Yet inmost, when he marked the Dahis there,
Standing,—a present wonder, uncompared,—
He cast upon a scheme for his revenge,
Or failing that, he meant to win by wile:
For with a certain sort, remorseless fraud
Works a more sweet revenge than noon-day blows!

Meanwhile the tribesmen urged their fretful steeds
To gain the far-off tents; but on their ears
The voice of Antar's brother loudly cried:—
" O tribes of Abs and Adnan, aye, and ye
" Of Dibyan and Fazarah, hear me now;
" For I will speak a little!—Ye have heard
" Of every word declared about this race,
" The praise of Dahis and the peerless mare?—
" Howbe, I think to battle those twain steeds
" Running apace upon that very course,

" Sans further stipulation, Sirs, than this :
" If-so I win, those hundred beasts are mine ;
" And if I lose,—I give up fifty beasts ? "
And they all laughed at him, then went their ways !—

But Antar when he heard his brother's words,
Deemed him a trifler; yet because he knew
That no mere man could worst him in a race,
Drew nigh to him with others of his tribe,
And thereupon addressed him : "O Shiboob,
" Son of a heathen mother, make it plain
" How thou can'st do this—how out-vie two steeds
" Elected by the chieftains of the tribes
" From all the chosen glories of their stalls,—
" Things like the wind and fleeter than most birds ? "—
Whereat Shiboob : " Describe them as you list ;
" I have out-sped a sandgrouse often-times,
" Rising out of its silver dune, perdiê !
" Belike I will outreach your ridden steeds ;
" And generous profit, unforeseen of these,
" Will so accrue to me ; for when my name
" Is blazoned through Arabia, in mischance
" No foe will venture far in my pursuit
" Once having caught the open." Antar smiled :
Then rode with those about him to the King,
With whom he supped right merrily, I ween ;
And with attuned adventure eased the night.

But as to Hadifah, Ill-crowning Dark
That strewed sweet balm upon the trancèd lids
Of Antar and the King, dealt him disquiet !
Wherefore at midnight from his cheerless tent
He crept out snakishly across the camp :—
Anon met Dhamis, chief among his slaves ;
And beckoning him, he took him thence aside,
Whispering :—" O Dhamis, I have oft-times heard

" On many a tongue the praise of thy fair deeds ;
" Yet luckless never had I need of thee
" To honour thee with my behest, till now."
Then Dhamis louting low : " My lord speak on ;
" And whatsoever you desire of me,
" If it be possible, it shall be done ! "
Hadifah, soft : "Suppose the deed were red ! "
(Hinting to slay the king); whereat the slave :
" I will do aught for thee less one sole deed !
" My lord still loves the king ? " " Nay not the king,
" Nor any man, thou foolish one ! Now mark :—
" To-morrow witnesses this race of ours ;
" My name and fame are poised on victory ;
" And ridicule on loss out-stings the loss.
" Therefore, away, and take the great defile,
" And hug the dappled rocks beside the course.
" Mark well the horses as they hie thereto ;
" And if accursèd Dahis holds afront,
" Bolt at him ; strike him ; make him start astray !—
" Then Ghabra will out-pace him, and reproach
" Will quickly fly us by this foiled defeat ! "
But Dhamis wonderingly to him replied,
" So-be, my Lord ! yet when in storms of dust
" These coursers near me, what shall be my sign
" Whereby to ken which steed displeases thee ? "
Then Hadifah, " This thing is easy too ;
" For Ghabra has her standard to that spot ;
" And will not fail ! Now, take this bag of stones !—
" When first the sun uplifts, use four of them :
" Withhold not throwing till two-thirds are thrown
" And it will be the Ghabra coming by !
" Oppose her not ; nay, bid her speed amain :
" For she will surely win : but look : anon !—
" If but a fourth, or any number less
" Be cast forth at your hand, arise ; beware !

" Dahis leads on the day : rush out at him !
" Turn him toward the desert : All is ours !—
" And thou shalt earn a rare reward of us :—
" Whereof I give this fair assurance now."
So Dhamis stole aside across the dark,
And lay among the grey rock till'the morn.

What time the Pleiads paled to secret gold
Adown the dawnrise, from all winds of heaven
New throngs of horsemen came like random clouds
Toward the level reaches by the lake ;
Where-by, reflected in the rippled flood,
Quaffing the early breeze, the Dahis stood,—
Kept by a golden rein ; while thence aloof,
Beside her master, pasturing her eyes,
On every least vague stir of ease he made,—
Ghabra the lean-flanked mare went beautiful,
Wooing the Morning with her sheeny neck :
And all the long lake whispered merrily,
As if no morn so sweet had kissed its face
Since erst it charmed the fair stars with its love,—
Lapping the silver shallows till the din
Of myriad voices hushed its music dumb.
But ere the first ray peeped along the plain,
The lusty clamour fell ; for thitherward
Amid their friends went Antar and the king ;
While from beside them, toward his starting-point
Shiboob, like some lithe antelope, went forth :
And all men wondered at his seemlyhed :—
Albeit curious at his strange conceit,—
Dreaming to triumph o'er such nimble steeds !

Eftsoons, resembling some resplendent shield
Whose dazzling field out-lightens all its charge,
The golden orb uprose and started them ;

Whereat each jockey gave a gallant shout ;
And like an ostrich urging with the gale,
Shiboob stole forth behind them, and the course,—
As when an eyot in the midst a stream,
Immersed in rain-risen waters, from each side
Falls strip by strip between them till quite lost,—
Became a headlong, variegated flood,
Lustily roaring.   But of them that stood
Far from the start, full soon it was well seen
That Ghabra held the front of those two steeds ;
Wherefore the hasty Fazarèan said :—
" Ye are thrown out, ye men of Abs : "   Again :—
" Comfort yourselves in grief."   Then they, enfierced,—
" Ye lie, O Fazarèans ; tarry yet.—
" Wait till they reach the mead ; for shingly ground
" Such as they cover now, befriends a mare ! "
Then forthwith Dahis left the faltering mare
Labouring bravely : while like fleet gazelle,
Shiboob kept stedfastly before them both,
Until they gained the verge of that defile
Where baleful treachery (worse than savage war
Or open fight though fierce), awaited them.
For Dhamis, that vile slave, had barely cast
A fourth those fateful stones away, ere-when
He lifted up his snake-eyes and descried
The Absian courser quickening on Shihoob
Well to the fore : whereat he gripped a flint,
And dashing forward smote him o'er the eyes,
Shouting amain to drive him back again :
So that the hurt steed staggered wilderedly
Shedding a little crimson flower of ease
Out of his wound upon the silver sand,
And well-nigh lost his rider.   But Shiboob
Hearing a cry, looked round,—and in his mind
Grasping the deed as Hadifah's, ran back,

And darting falcon-wise upon the slave,
Snatched his own knife, and smote him through˙ the ribs,
So that the dastard swooned to dismal death,
Slaking the frolic dust that flitted up
In little mocking wreaths and fell again
Upon his moveless corse :—then sped aside
To coax the piteous courser; thereupon
Tearing along the level, Ghabra came.
While keen Shiboob, afraid to lose his beasts,
Played with his feet again toward the lake,
And flew among the plaudits of the throng
Two arrow-flights afront the rauting mare
Even as gust of heaven ! But far aloof,
Led by the jockey, Káis marked his steed
Panting toward him ; yet the while it came,
Shiboob fore-shewed the deed ; and therewithal
The whole crowd murmured like the angry sea ;
And Antar dashed his hand upon his hilt,
Looking a thousand deaths, this way and that ;
Longing to ease his vengeance on the tribe
That used the carrion Jackal ; But the Sheikhs
Entreated patience of him, and went forth,
And spake to Hadifah, reviling him :—
He straight forswearing knowledge of the deed,
Demanding ragefully the victor's prize ;—
Which they denied him, favouring more Shiboob !
So all that day they went among the chiefs
Quenching the smouldering tumult : for the sword
Hissed in the scabbard, and the hilt was hot.
But for the King, his sweet revolted heart
Had well-nigh broke, o'erfraught with chained-up Rage,
Had not they Twain remained to comfort him,
Swearing by Zuhayr's tomb to wreak revenge
Upon the crew of traitors, and the man
Who so devised the race for deadly ends.

Albeit the victor merry with his prize,
Slaughtered full twenty head and made a feast
Among the maimed and straitened of his tribe;
Keeping the eighty other for the stalls.
And these were not the only beasts he won:
For he was as the eagle of the land!

But when the chieftains of Fazàrah heard
How Antar's brother took their peerless beasts,—
The treasures of their pen,—and hewed them up
To banquet the mere beggars of his tribe,
They murmured peevishly, as children do
That watch their hard-given toys unkindly used:
As if the giver swayed the gift foregone;—
And the more shameless thronged to Hamil's tent
Buzzing like angry wasps; but found him not;
Then issuing forth they met the brothers twain
Coming toward them; while not far afoot,
Hassan, (the elder's son),—the star elect
Of all their golden youth—the fairest flower
That wizard Fate e'er drew from venomed root,—
Held earnest audience with an ancient Sheikh;
Who with heart-swelling remnant of sweet voice,
Musicked some antique legend richly-dight;
And while the soft air swept the old man's beard,
Spraying its gentle Silver to the sun,
Hadifah came between them, quivering, pale,
Urging his son: "Quick! get you gone to Abs;
" Commend their King to pay the pledge we won;
" Or by the sun in heaven, we come to take it!"
Whereat the hoary Sheikh, with eyes aglow
Beneath his solemn brow like wells of fire,
Broke fox-like through the little wire of word,
" Nay, will not this large air be sore ascorn
" To waft such insult to the men of Abs?
" They are our cousins :—should have courteous use!

" The King has done no outrage.   Nay, make Peace :
" For fierce affliction whelms the stubborn will !
" Consider thy vile slave who smote their steed,—
" And how the knife of swift-avenging doom
" Left him a shrivelled mass upon the sand,—
" Stained with the awful colour of his deed !—
" Take graft of mellowed counsel that thy works
" May bring thee sweet reward ! "—The other then,
Not daring, though enraged, to strike the man,
Fluttering his lissom fingers, called him ' Dog ' :
And swore to leave no Absian tent unreaped,
Were the whole plain sewn thick with them like stars,—
An Káis would not send the camels back !
Howbeit the patient Elder cried aloud :—

      " Outrage inglorious
        Unawares openeth
        Out on the innocent,
        Like a marauder
        Using the darkness.
        Clothe not thyself Thou
        Eldest of Zaalim,
        With raiment of infamy !
        Hear from Themood,
        The ever-informed-well,—
        How from a single
        Evening of Summer,
        All the rebellious—
        Youthly and beautiful --
        Terribly slaughtered,
        Lay in the morning—
        Their dim eyes entreatfully
        Glaring on Heaven :—
        Watched of the vulture,
        A feast for the leopard ! "-·

                      E

Hadifah, scoffing, led the lad away,
Bidding him forth to Abs upon the quest
Even as he said. And He obeying, went.

So through the night rode Hassan till the morn
Charged all the tinctless plain with waving gold
That dazzled up toward the azure heaven,
(As if they gave sweet challenge like two Knights
That find each other friends, and so pass by,
Having saluted),—when the Absian tents
Broidered their fair battalions on the sky
Like even pearls ; and ere distressful heat
Drew foam upon his steed, he well discried
The sunward tent of Káis, half-engirt
By guardian tribesmen : but the King was forth.
Straightway he bowed obeisance at the door
Keeping the jewelled reins within his hand :
For, like the Moon amid her chaste white stars,
Modelilah among her maids came out :
And he awaiting not her gentle word
(The warm flood rising freshly to his face),
Excused himself and questioned of the King :
While She, half-losing the sweet married rose
On her fair cheeks, surveying that bright face
With all its golden curls uncapped before her,
Asked him in sudden pause of stately walk :—
" What would'st thou, an the King were here ?" Then he,
Shewing reluctant shame :—" O noble Queen,
" My father sent me to demand our due :
" The hundred camels wagered on the race ! "—-
Whereat compassion awed her merry voice,
Turning its silver to a tender hush
Purling response :—" Alas, thou heedless youth !
" Dost thou not fear such errand ?—Save thyself !
" For chanced it that the King beheld thee here,

" On such a message, he would send thee forth
" Into a starless, dawnless sleep Beyond ! "—
Then he, more governed by her queenly grace
Than by her counsel, turned him silently,—
Waving a mute farewell,—and went his way :
So, once more saw the threaded stars arise
Over the lake of Oorah from the hills,
Ere yet he viewed his father's face again,
Coming to greet him.
                    Then he told him all :—
How that the King was forth a-hunting gone,
And what Modèlilah his Queen, had said.
Hadifah reddening, stormed and called him ' Fool ! '
' A thrall of Women ! '—bidding him go back
And clinch the business or return no more.
So Hassan took his welcome sleep that night
Within his father's tent ; then sleeping dreamed
Of that sweet Queen, and saw both Death and Love
Passing before him ; yet at morning-tide
Rose blithe in all the bounty of his years.

    Now when the King drew home, and overnight
Sat in his tent at ease and heard the songs
Of gentle minstrel charming the stilled air,
Modèlilah went thither all alone,
And told him how the Fazarean sent
Demanding courteously, to take his due,—
' The Hundred camels ! '—But the King astart,
Rose like a storm of thunder, shook the tent,
And swore an oath, he would have slain the man.
Then, calming for the cloud of rage removed,—
" ' Tis over ; let it pass ! "—and hummed again,
Catching a melody loved long ago ;
And seemed at peace, and kissed her on her eyes.

Howbeit he sorrowed in his sleep that night.
But when the dawnrise shot each chink with gold,
As emulous to rouse the tristful King,
Toward that proud pavilion, Antar came :
And Káis rose to meet him, and retold
How Hadifah sent his son, and on what quest ;
Repeating sore :—" I would have killed the man ! "
When Antar hearkening, glanced without the door,
Wherein, with all the sunny glow of youth
Came gentle Hassan, unsaluting, calm
Meeting their startled gaze with simple words :—
" O king, my father sends me for his due :—
" The hundred wagered camels ; otherwise
" Affliction mounts against you : and mishap
" May leave less with you than you now deny ! "—
But at the threat, within the mild King's eyes,
The azure day grew dark, and all the storm
Of inward rage eclipsed his lordlier face ;
And ere the hapless One might use his rein,
A cruel javelin smote him thro' the breast,
And issuing left him falling from his steed
When Antar caught him.   So they took a thong
And bound him to his horse, and turned the beast
Round to the westward, urging it with whips,
Till like a bird, it lessened in their view,
And the horizon mingled it with beams.

What time the dayset scattering evil clouds
Flamed in the rainlit pastures, and the air
With unseen finger smoothed the tumbled flowers,
The Fazarean shepherds from their cotes
Beheld the steed of Hassan far aloof,
Grazing riderless ; so they gat to horse,
And circling warily, viewed the fearful deed,—
The bright defenceless hair uncurled for blood,

Too heavy for the evening breeze to lift,
Adown the courser's crimson flank ;—the face
Like a narcissus shewing to the heaven ;
While both his stiffened hands hung down one way ;
And o'er the strong right hand a vermeil streak,
Stained the dead waxen nails :—nor did the steed
Disown its masters, but stood feeding on,
Steamy with toil : and thus they led it home
Bearing the piteous load upon its back
Unto his father's tent—O sight of woe !—
Beneath the dolorous twilight, whose sweet stars
Seemed to be gathering from the inmost heaven,
As tho' they heard the little whispering steps
That took the silent band along the grass,—
Or would come down to garland Beauty dead !
But their soft beams could shine no more for him,
Never so bright be they :—So those men went
Moaning a dirge before a childless tent,
The sire forth-hurrying thence to know the thing,—
Smiting his breast ; then weeping streams of fire :
So that his fox-face shone in sore constraint
Under the running tears : he crying aloud :—
" To Arms, Fazarah ! Rise, revenge your Child !
" Leave not a tent along the Tyrant's camp
" Ere this fell hour to-morrow !"
                          Then distraught,
Sprang to the crimson corse, and in his arms
He, kneeling down, upraised it,—passionately
Kissing the wareless lips.—So all that night
A noise of eager swords and grinding spears
Hissed in the windless air ; and on the morn
The whole tribe, (save the women and the sick),
Immersed in brilliance, like a sea of steel,
Rode to the sunset slowly, like a storm

Of beetling thunder uttering muffled growls ;—·
And rested neath the stars.   But ere the Dawn
Blazed its gold arrows at retiring Dark,
The air was as a whirlwind-woof of sand ;
Whence lightnings of disastrous scimitars
Shot like a thousand shuttles, or like stars
Which weep destruction o'er the fields of Night :—
So that the firm plain reeled in dire convulse
Shaken with deafening tumult, frantic, hurled,
That mocked the shrilling trump ; and like a flame
The heart of Antar leapt within his breast,
Spreading a glorious heat thro' all his frame,
Till, like a high-plumed billow of the deep
When the sun strikes it hurrying to the shore,
Out to the fight he rode ; and Káis the King,
Drew close beside him ; while, ere battle joined,
From the opposing field, arrayed like Night,
Spectral with grief the son of Zaalim came ;—
Crying : "O son of Zuhayr, was it well
"To slay a tender youth,—the sole sweet flower
"Of my down beaten heart ; O coward King !
"And thou his bastard-knight !—it was enough
"That Thou should'st stain thy doubly-royal hands
"In blameless blood, and not have given to Him
"The right of an unsacred touch : but some
"Beheld him bind the stiff thong round the limbs,
"More like relentless fiend : yet well it is
"To come forth thiswise to a field of spears
"That shall proclaim anon which one of us
"O'er this land holds dominion ? "—Therewithal,
Out from beneath his standard rushed the King
Springing toward the chieftain ; and the day
Grew black with mutual fury fore their eyes
Mingling them like two clouds ; while dreadful shouts
Dinned in the air mid clash of myriad spears ;

And Antar down the midst hewed right and left,
Mowing even as a scythe mows ;—hands and heads
Spinning like plane-leaves in the autumn-time ;—
So that himself, his armour, and his horse,
Like some great scarlet standard waved along,
Purfled and branched with gore.   But for the King,
Working terrible things, his foe anon
Dealt him a grievous hurt along the hip,
Grazing the bone ; but therewith lost his sword :
Whereat the King closed on him, like a lion,
Gripping with all his main the brazen rings
Upon the corselet, and so flung him off
Clear to the ground, leaving him spoiled for dead :
Without his massy spear and heron-plume.
Then Antar pressed back even as he went,—
More like a molten torrent sweeping trees
And crops of golden grain before its course,
Than like the living semblance of mere Man.
Wherefore the warriors fell about the King,
Hurried on helplessly, wounded :—some being borne
By the dire tumult dead long ere they fell !

Thus Káis won the fight : for ere that eve,
The host of Fazareans fled away
E'en like a cloud of locusts ; and the plain
Where they went forth was strewn with dying men,
And blind hurt steeds that heard the vulture's wing
Fluttering around, and trembled ; and the dust
Smoked in the starlight as the King returned.
There was no battle like it in his land
In all the days of Káis : and long since
Veteran warriors love to tell the deeds
Of Antar, and the valour of the King !—

1882.

THE DEATH OF ANTAR.[*]

PART I.

*A Rocky place near a deep ravine, over which the early
dawn throws an increasing brilliance on the ancient
trunks of an adjacent forest.   Enter a chorus of
white-robed maidens which divides equally, and then
breaks into alternate music.*

CHORUS I.

Far, far is the Winter's cold,
   And the days of the long decline ; ·
   The flowers are abrim with wine
Of the morn and ablaze with its gold ;
And the cinnamon odour is borne, as of old,
   On the breath of the morning, divine :
     While Heaven unbinds
From afar the fetters of all the streams ;
   And the light-footed clouds beloved of the winds,
Like the shadowless shapes of immortal dreams,—
     Dissolve in its beams.

CHORUS II.

For the strains of Sorrow have faded away ;
   Our hearts are filled as with light ;
And the song of the sun-girt herald of Day
   Is abroad in the azure height ;
While the Angel of Love glides softly down
   From her throne in the sapphire Heaven ;
And flower-sweet things from her lips are blown,
   And manifold graces are given.

---

[*] A short edition of this poem was issued two years ago. It is
here however, in a re-written and, I trust, amended form.

Chorus I.

For the Spirit of Spring within every leaf
  Inspires the smile of the April hours ;
And the mother of seasons arisen from Grief
  Unfolds the wings of her angel flowers ;
        And all sweet bowers
Enkindle the love of the birds that alight,
  And awaken the song that divides and devours
The lips and the innermost heart of the Night
      With desire and delight.

Chorus II.

Sing aloud, thou flowering Grove
  For the lilies of Gladness appear ;
Coo early and late, thou fond Ring-dove :
  Breathe soft in the Jonquil's ear :
For the breezes of Heaven are laden with Love
And the day of betrothal is here.

Chorus I.

May the bountiful angel of Fate scatter blessings as
    flowers in their way ;

For twain lovers true, are in bliss ; aye, more than
    married are They !

Chorus II.

He getteth her glory of heart : she giveth him joy to
    to command :– ·
She more than out-sweetening the Spring ;—He, peer-
    less, the Lord of the land.

Chorus I.

May each pasture and forest responsive, re-echo the
    strain that we sing:
Not alone this enshrouded ravine their vows be
    re-antheming !

Chorus II.

For Beauty too often, God wot,—is wedded to Lust and
    Pain,—
Soon emptied of Love and Delight, and enthralled by
    Regret and Disdain:
"For Good is attainless, they say ; and Wisdom—an Old
    Man's dream !"—
Even so are the blossoming boughs hurried down on the '
    darkening Stream.

Chorus I.

Yet Wisdom is lordship of Joy, and a glory it is to be
    strong ;
And allied by Love unto Beauty, these make Life likest
    to Song.

                [*Clouds overspread the sky*].

Chorus II.

No longer the music of morning entrances our listening
    ears ;—
Lo ! a ringing sound comes up,—as of eager encrossing
    of spears !

Chorus I.

And see how a rabble of vultures entangles in mid-way
  flight
Some steadfast imperial bird—the gloom of whose wing
  is as night :
Twice, thrice, hath he sundered their thickest; whole
  legions of slayers are slain,
And are falling inglorious afar to the pastureless face of
  the plain ;
While he wheels in their screaming,midst; then his wings
  flutter to and fro,
Shaken darkly aloose and aloft on the wind as the lost
  leaves go,
Till fainting, and spoiled of his pride, in a ruin of plumes
  doth he fall,
Whirled round, as if drunken with death,—his foes for a
  funeral pall !

Chorus II.

Alas ! this omen strange foretokens woe and ruth !
Hush ! Some-one comes this way, led by a Stranger-
  Youth !

  [Wezar *led by* Nedim *slowly emerges from the forest*].

Wezar.

The festal-notes of little forest birds,
Till now have sweetly fallen on my ears :
Till now, too, on these niggard lids the Night
Of Day withheld, has hung inexorably :
Howbe the endearing hints of present Morn
Send cheerier summons to my plealess heart.
Hark, too,—a song ! Ah ! what a joy is that ! --
Whence is the voice ?

NEDIM.

              O Master we are come
To the fast-lightening verge ; and on a lawn
Which the dew-glittering valley-rocks inclose,
Enlaurelled maidens, unregarding us,
Sparkle in merry dance.   A moment more,
And they will see us, too !—

WEZAR.

              It is some camp !
Are there no men there ?—

NEDIM.

           None —

WEZAR.

                What stills the song ?

NEDIM.

Seeing us coming :—likelier marking you
Engirded with these daggers—they have hushed
Their music so to freelier gaze at you !

WEZAR.

Was it a strain of merriment or praise ?
What last I caught seemed of more stately tone
Than doth become a dance.   Aye, tell me that !
For noonday being enshrouded from my sight,
My ear regards the very subtlest touch

Of sound : and by my ear, I hear and see;
And but divine divergences can warp
This doubly-sentient judge.   Go, bid them sing !

NEDIM.

Master, they look too fine an Kings should bid them !
How should they sing for me ?—

WEZAR.

Go to : be bold !

NEDIM.

They must have heart to sing from,—want a theme
And having these, they might not !

WEZAR.

Give them gold !
They'd sell their songs and bodies for a coin.
The singer like the maiden must be pressed :
For, vanity are both their yea and nay;
And with a little soft servility
Which is, as honey to the dancing-bear,
The surest barter for the trick with-held,—
You may command them even to extremes.

NEDIM.

Nay, your own eyes, were they your witnesses,
Would chide such thought unkind.—

WEZAR.

I'll not believe't,
Which is their tribe ?—but ask them of their song.

CHORUS.

See how they talk! Now mark, he sends the boy
To get some speech of us :—perchance our strain
Has scared their game past bowshot!

NEDIM

                        Gentle maids,
My chase-stained garb offends ye? nathëless,
I would not mar your song.

CHORUS.

            O civil knave!
Behold a gallant and well-spoken boy!
How-be, let's question of his Majesty!—
Look how he stumbles : mark : the man is mad!
                         [*To* NEDIM]
What man is he who quits those deepening shades,
And cometh like a blind one?—tell us boy!
Aye, be not shy!

WEZAR.

           In sooth, this I will tell—
When ye enliven us with tuneful song!

CHORUS.

Nay, let us flee: he frowns most gloomily!

WEZAR.

Ah! dread me not fair maids; I am so blind
Your beauty's light may this veil never pierce.

I have not seen a flower for five long years ;
And what I last saw was not Woman's face.
I heard your gentle music with delight :—

[*Aside*].

Me-fancied all the dreams of Youth returned,
And all the gleaming plain awave with flowers
Smiled in the sunrise ; while I saw my Love
Abla, daughter of Malik, my betrothed,
Singing beside the stream in Shurebàh !

[*To the Chorus*].

Perchance a stranger asks too much ?—

CHORUS.

We grudge no man our hero, nor his praise.

[*They sing in unequal time to tambour and cymbals*].

As for Him, his glory is seen in battle,
　　Spears like hurrying serpents around him hissing :—
Sundering blades and thundering hooves of chargers :—
　　　　Slayer of heroes !
On to their haunches he reins the thin-flanked coursers,
All the great plain reels as a storm-smitten vessel,
While he arrow-like, urgeth amid the foemen,—
　　　　Lion undaunted !

See : like lightning over the mountainous water,
Flashes his Indian sword ; and as leaves in the Autumn,
Fall the alien arms as he furrows onward,
　　　　Freer of Women !—

All his armour is dyed like the Judas-flower :
All the sand is aglow as with littering blossom :
While he cries on Abla, daughter of Malik,—
      Glory of maidens !

                  [Softlier].

And She his tender, eloquent, deer-eyed ABLA,
In her tent reclines like an island of spices.
Her glances are as the arrows of song to a Lover :
Sweet is her mouth as a chalice of exquisite flowers ;
Her cheeks resemble the peonies of the garden :—
      Glory of Women !

Pleasant her lips to kiss,—like the dew-written roses :
Tyrannous tresses rill from her blue-veined temples :
And when a Mortal, sorrowing, gazes upon Her,
      Rapture inflames him.

      [The echo dies away in the ravine.]

        WEZAR.

Abla, my cousin ?— Aye !—but who is he ?—

        CHORUS.

Antar his name is : Abla is his spouse.

      WEZAR.   *[Suddenly infuriate.*

God's light I I dream, or hideous frenzy takes me ?—
      [The chorus flee behind the rocks and trees.

Quick ! string my bow : and Hell inspire my arm !
> [*When they are in safety, Nedim gives him the bow.*]

Now may I strike the same—
> [*He shoots an arrow that strikes a tree.*]

NEDIM.
> O master, hold.

CHORUS.
Thou fool ! a tree may bear well short of an axe !

WEZAR.   [*more deliberate.*]
This is the shaft I never loosed in vain !

NEDIM.
Master, they shift them in such nimble-wise,
You might use swords as sagely on their song
As these good arrows on their safe retreat :
For they are peeping at you from the rocks,
And mocking from behind dark cedar-trunks !

WEZAR.
Silence, you clown !—your noise unwhets my ear !
Quickly, an arrow !—Now !

NEDIM.
> Ah ! stay your hand !

WEZAR.
Lightning deprive their lips !—O name thrice-damned !—
And hath my wanton cousin for his bride ?—
It is too hard !—Nay, was it not enough,

F

A despot, near whom, Death should seem a friend,
Beside whose hell-hued valour-seeming face
The ugliest, most deformed, divorcèd thing
In all the Catalogue of Nature's work,
Would seem within the eye of my revenge
As Beauty's self.—O most Incarnate Hell!—
Ingloriously robbed me of my sight,
And stung my soul with bitterest agonies?
And now, from my own kin, the loveliest girl,
The very sweet distilment of all grace,
Hath ta'en to get him joy ;—aye, one, of whom,
From childhood's dawn,—I hold remembrances!—
Why should I stay my hand?—Who speaks to me?—
I will be firmer than the unyielding rock
That doth not shake tho' whirl-winds rage at it,
And as the thirsty torturing tiger,—cruel !—

CHORUS.

O thrice-skilled vaunter ; self-deceiving fool !
Thy bearing might have made thee fair report
In suchwise as mere seeming of a man :
Though not ill-spent was this mad savagery,
If thou hast learned that thy exultant skill,
Is vain, opposed to Song !—Go : get thee hence !—
Cousins may be more bitter for their bond !—

NEDIM.

O Master, hold !

CHORUS.

     The fool would slay us all :
And merely that we sang a Hero's praise :
That too, being at his bidding !

WEZAR.

        Help me hell !—

What sound was that ?—Aha ! methinks one falls !
My wit is nimbler than your wise man's saw.
[*Derision from the Chorus.*]

NEDIM.

Beseech thee, Master, hold ; not they are hurt :—
A little bird was winging tree to tree,
When your fierce arrow smote him, and the plumes,
[*The chorus flee down the ravine.*]
Like little waifs of dead men's characters,
In tiny travelling clusters whirled adrift,
Are being borne toward us by the breeze.

WEZAR.

You have too much of feeling in your soul
For worthy use ; 'twere best you get you gone :
I have no need of you.

NEDIM.

Heaven help You then !
Have I not wrongs like yours that cry for blood ?
Did not this Antar stab the breast that nursed me,—
Even my own dear mother, as they tell ?
Did he not turn the children's hair to grey,
What time athwart the dawn he took our tribe,
Tearing the guardian tents to bloody shreds ?—
But do I anger out at idle straws,
Or wear a shapely grief to scornèd rags ?—

WEZAR.

Enough, 'twas damnèd, and his own day will come.
Nay, talk not of yourself : but swear by Heaven
Ere I be quit of you, to lead me near him :
For then I surely know we shall not fail.
I will not ask you for another mock,
Nor curse thee for thy craftier indolence :

Nay! wander onward, like some common brook,
Washing the casual weeds that give you shade.
'Tis but a devil can outwit the Blind
When he perceives a danger in their path!—

NEDIM.

Feeble indeed are they to aid themselves!
Remember you when those too cruel chains
Ate with their bitter rust into your limbs,
I, only I, did tend your least desires,
And with this breath becooled your smarting lids,
And stayed no speech to beg new favourings,
Though at my peril!

WEZAR.

        Cease your shameless boast! .
To gloss your good deed is to dull its worth
And turn its beauty to a painted show.
Is my breast hairless?—Tell me, braggart boy,
Where has the Tyrant camped? no idle words!—
Place unto place, as promise unto promise,
Ever-delaying, with excuse replete,—
Talking for deeds, yet shrinking from occasion,—
You long have led me.   But the hour has come
When there shall be an end to your deceits.
Point me the soft place of his jubilee,
And I will, as some blithe, home-wending bird,
Into his green nest dip my poisonous wings,
And greet him, e'en with Death's contagious kiss,
Who most,—for doing me that deed accursed,
For Sin's own sake,—I love; or by God's light,
This Earth knows you no more!

      [WEZAR *seizes him violently, but releases him.*

NEDIM.

              It is most false:
I never did deceive you,—thankless wretch!

WEZAR.

Here, take this gold : it is your lawful hire.
Nay, I'll not hurt you.   Say my words were harsh.
I know you have done many things for me,
Wherefore I give you gold : Aye boy, be friends !
Am not I blind?

NEDIM.

Far abler armèd then,
To guard the looseness of each other sense.—

WEZAR.

The fledgling imitates the full-grown bird !
Use simpler words boy, and less sentiment.
I am too old to care for moral saws,
And you too young to use them natively !
Hence ; for the sun must now be high-advanced.

NEDIM.

If he should seize us prowling near his camp?—
I dread to think.—Death were the least for You !

WEZAR.

If this wide-ranging lithe ambassador
By your help shall find Him,—How fares it then ?—

NEDIM.

I have but little hope.

WEZAR.

Go to : get more :
At your age, hope should silver every hour :
Like lambs-wool on the brakes ere shearing-time.

NEDIM.

What we do then, will be the last we do !—

WEZAR.

Then do it well ; tis best done that's done true.

NEDIM.

Well, since you are confirmed, I'll doff my mask,
And shew you what a cunning seer revealed me.—

[Drawing close to WEZAR.]

There is a green nook by a mighty stream :
   Euphrates is its name, renowned in song :
   Lithe willows lean from either bank along;
Beneath, the river glides, like one in dream.
And from its farther side the silvery gleam
   Of happy tents relumes the evening sky :
   Like little stars they glance up merrily,
While Comfort from each door doth sweetly beam.
Beyond them, rise the giant mountains old,
   Whose great feet gird the widening plain below
   Where wet, blown grasses like the billows flow,
Revealing in their wave the height so cold.
There sleeps the bridegroom by his tender bride,
   There cleave the faithful lips of love this night;
   There Antar revels in Love's dear delight,
Where foes are none, and Abla is his Pride.

WEZAR.

God's light, I hear those harlots yelling still !—
Come, leave them to their daylight fooleries,
Hence, away !—   *[Exeunt.]*

PART II.

Twilight.   The banks of an arm of the Euphrates.

NEDIM.

Master, our toil is finished.   We are come
Unto an open place anear the stream ;
And all the plain along the farther side
Is patterned out in little silver peaks :
Where, too, the lonely snows are gathered up
Into the loftier mountains far beyond,
The fallen sun has left them all aflush,
Like a wide linn of Love's elysian flowers ;—
While in the eddies of the raven river,
I can see glimmering fruits, new-lighted there,
Hurrying helpless toward the bitter sea :
And tiny bats are gadding to and fro
Tangling the dark and light.

WEZAR.

What sound is that ?–

NEDIM.

Lo, yonder stands a lordlier tent than all !
And in the garden of its silvery skirt,
Feeds a slim courser sabler than the night ;
And from the grassy sod, enfixed aslant,
Lifts a dark spear whose over-peering point
Glimmers like Sirius seen behind a mist :—
And thither wind two streams of maidenhood

Bearing dim harps enwreathed with snowy flowers,
Which they seem tuning.

WEZAR.

          Nedim, what you see
Is Antar's tent; and that proud courser, past
A doubt, the ebon Abjar :—(*Aside*) and the lance
That span me thrice along the loathsome dust.
Yea, thrice I've rolled before the crimson feet
Of that dark steed ; for which our viperous tribe
Scorns me as one cast out.
        [*Lifting his head, and turning to the camp, in
                      suppressed voice.*]
           Eternal night
Forever round me ! Never in sweet sleep
Can these maimed eyelids close as once they closed
In golden boyhood.—No delightful flowers
Illume this Loveless wilderness of mine,
Only the dripping of their dews I hear,
Or when the wind just makes a sweet disturb,
Sighing among the swaying cypress-trees !
Though thou hast Paradise in every rose ;
And Love with Spring-time—which is Heaven itself !
But Fortune now enfavouring my kept vow
Shall give thee death, thou tyrant, by this hand,—
This little mortal hand that fears not Thee :
Nor shook not when hot rods were simmering up
The very light of all the gentle world.
Play on thy wanton playings : ease the sighs
Of her thy Love-mate : sleep on her white breast,
If so thy hell-black locks still lie ungreyed :—
Let thy words meet like Lovers, in her soul ;
For if this little weeping Breeze speak true,
There shall be echoes to its infant sob,
Among these willows : and in Death's cold court

Thou wilt not find kind lips to greet thy kiss
Nor proud white arms that mimic crushing thee ;
Nor in the gritty depth unseen of Day,
Among the noiseless creep of battening worms,
(Whose monarch is King Death, the God of change),—
Wilt thou meet blisses worthy of true Love ?—
Outbrim, I say, the shallow cup of joy,
Thro' whose clear wine the lees of woe are seen ;
For by the evil in Man's heart, I swear,—
Even as God's thunder by the lightning swears,—
There shall be whisper of tears ; and Bitterness
Shall cry against these hours. Heaven's curse fulfilled,
Haply thy grief may make it purge thy sin !
For if this venom o'er thy vaunted might

> [*He dips an arrow into a phial.*]

Have mastery, thou'lt surely grieve to death,
And topple from thy noon-height into Hell ! ! !
Give me to drink !—too much joy kills like pain !

> *   *   *   *   *   *   *   *

Now lead me on a little, to some spot
Which on thy oath doth lie opposed his tent
So aptly that no shaft may fail to smite
A nestling-bird—should it make chirping thence !

NEDIM.

Master I will.   The quiver has but One !—
And the best bow,—already strung.—Now here
The tent-door opens clearly toward your face :—
A little lower :—thus :—I'll hide aloof,—

> [*Going aside—then reluctantly stopping a moment.*]

Now doth the little fire-fly shed his gleam,
Making a tiny glory as he wings !
So does the soul shine, when the body fades,
Wandering among those bowers of Bliss up there.—

O hark,—those maidens offering songs of peace !
How sweet, were I a partner in their joys :—
Not leading random life without all hope,—
Less than the Thistles' down upon the wind !
Their strings do seem to catch the river's tone
Measuring its gentle spirit to these stars :
One might imagine all its depth aglow,—
Even beneath the shade those dark isles throw ?—
Now mazy troubles gather in their harps,
Which are not in their song :—

WEZAR.

> Go to : mad boy !
Else they will hear these civil ecstacies !—
Stay !—let this music physic me the while.
Haply in my ears it will sweetlier speak
Than in yon vaunting Tyrant's.   Hark, again !—

SONG (*from over the River*).

Under a tent of glimmering leaves,
　Fond as a brooding dove,
On the river-breast softly heaves
The fairy Lotus-flower, and weaves
　Her own sweet dream of Love.

II.

And all the ancient River-song
　Lingereth round her like a dream ;
And all the emulous currents throng
To catch her love as they eddy along,—
　Lady of Life's wide Stream !

III.

Like a radiant wisp in the azure day ;
　Like a star on the sapphire height ;

Like a blossom aglow in the bright spring-way ;—
Like a sudden joy in a life gone grey,
  Is this flower of Earth's delight !

IV.

When the odourless children of the fields
  Grow dim, or fall to the mower;
The Angel of Love this one flower shields
From the sharp red sword that the Season wields,
  And endues it with power.

V.

A virtue remains in its virginal mien
  That maketh the hurt heart whole :
On the face of a sky where no star is seen,
It smiles—like peace after battle hath been,—
  This sweet Flower of the Soul !—

PART III.

SCENE I.   *On the further side.   Within the tent of
          Antar.   Early night.*

ABLA.

Lo Love, upon the softly-closing harps
Clouds are come up !—The strain they gave methought
Something too tristful, seeing we look for Joy :—
Albeit sweet enough.

ANTAR.

An ancient tune :
I heard it sung in Persia at the Court ;
And I remember that the bard who made it,
Wandering among the gardens, said to me :—
The swallows twittering round us as we talked,—
"The inspiration of true Song is sad :
And the divinest Love, not otherwise."—
Yet for the bettering of our merriment
To-morrow night let there be mirth and dance :
So Sweet, we shall be suited.

ABLA.

Truth, sweet Love !—
And I would almost now have asked for them,
But that musicians of the melting kind,
Being in this mood, would take it for misprize ;—
Seeing they deem their choice, lord Absolute,
And we, not peers, but plastic listening slaves.
There was a time ere erst our glorious tribe
By many foes oppressed, grew poor and weak,
That merry music winged the happy words,
And every voice entuned the general joy,—
Seeing we scarce knew sorrow.—But, look you :
Since we have borne a hard captivity,
Though by your valour, being, at last, enfreed,
And cheered with peace more than we whilom were,
Our poets trim lean dirges and strange cares ;
And for sweet mirth we sing clipt tragedies !—
Love, can'st thou call those other songs to mind ?—

ANTAR.

And has there flown a day I dared forget
Since first we loved,—since first I kissed you Love ?—

The precious days of Love are like the Sun
That shadows half the world and pales the stars :
They do out-dark the dark days ; while the bright
Are lost in greater glory.

WEZAR (*beyond*).
Love,—the accursed !

ABLA.

Then may you Sweet, recall that little song
Laid by your gentle hands amid the flowers
That gardened-round the tent at Jelilel ?—

ANTAR.

Yea Love. yet can I not call back the lines.
My soul hath since been uttered more, I think,
Through Battle than through veils of tender Song.
Yet this their spirit was—(*Kisses her*).

WEZAR (*faintly*).
O tyrant damned !—

ABLA.

My maidens wrought for it this silken frame,
And they have learned it.   Listen Love ; they'll sing

SONG.

I.

Thy damsels are as the wild-flowers sweet,
  But Thou art as Love's bud-rose
Whose innocent lips of their own joy meet
  When the wings of the Night unclose :
  And no virtue untold that the violet knows,
Nor the treasure of no white garland I weet,—
  May dare to emulate Those !

II.

I lifted away thy fragrant veil,
　　O Abla, thou fairest-born ;
And thy breath was soft like the Syrian gale,
　　And thy sweet face like the Morn.
　　And ah ! with thy smile, my bosom forlorn,
Like the voice of the passionate nightingale,
Like the midnight torn with glimmering hail—
　　By the demon of rapture was torn !

　　　　　　　　　[A great baying of the camp-dogs].

ANTAR (*rising*).

The watch-dog bays! Some prying pard, perchance ?—
They do not use to bay so suddenly :—
I will bespeak the captain of the watch.

ABLA (*entreatingly*).

Prithee O my sweet Lord ! Those dogs do bay
On every night with questioning the Moon ;
Who doth assume with her replenished light,
Uneven visage and fantastic shape
To work upon their fond, unreasoned eyes.
O do not leave me !—let me go with you !

ANTAR.

Nay, child, but let me forth ; nor for Love's sake
Forget the peril that may lurk around !—

　　　　　　　　　　　　　　[softlier].

Are there not foes 'neath Night's indifferent wing
As there are Loves and Angels ?

ABLA.

　　　　　　　Yet, sweet Love,
Should fiends affright us—angels being at hand ?
Hark, how the sound has wandered !

ANTAR.
                                Gentle Sweet,
I shall be back ere you can know me gone !

ABLA.

And He is gone,—and Abla could not stay him ?—
I will look forth !—The moon is travelling fast
Behind a massy continent of cloud :
Night on her envious quest has issued forth
And blotted out those fair-engrailed stars.
The bulbul sings no more !—But yonder see
A broad impetuous beam breaks through the cloud
And bathes the feet of the far-distant hills !—
There will be rain ere Morning smiles again !—
Ah me, what is that cry ?—It was his voice !

ANTAR (*faintly*).

Alas ! and in the darkness !

ABLA.

                                Hark ! he moans—
As if he sorrowed that sweet night is here ?
Speak but one word to guide me, Love ; I come !!!
                                [*She goes out*].

SCENE II.   *An open place by the river's bank.   The
                    baying at intervals.*

ANTAR.

Out, thou keen thief !—There, let it be thy shame
Dire perjured shaft to grovel on the plain ;
Though thy sleek lineaments do woo the air
To let thee emulate with transient speed

The royal Lightning's self! And thou out there,
Whose dastard fingers plied them at my voice,
Hoping to thrive by my unnoting ways ; —
Would that mine eyes might cleave this night to thee ;
That I might wither with one glance of scorn
Thy vile degenerate limbs,—O fitting feast
For the rank carrion-fowls that led thee here !
Was the high Sun too scornful of thy deeds ?
Would not the patient Moon admit thy prayer
(Loathing too much to be enleagued with Hell),
That thou successless coward, in thy soul
Hast made black covenants with hindering Night
To slay me here ?—not as a valorous foe
Who would outface an hundred made like thee
In the just Noon,—his back against his heart :
But me—a weaponless, unreckoning man ?
Were this same night full fifty times as thick,
Its breath out-stilling the lone wilderness,
It would seem sweet, and rival the bright Noon—
Compared with that dark traitorous heart of thine !
Still, deem not so to 'scape thy greedy Doom !
For were this little Stream to know once more
Its ancient universal might ere dawn,—
It should not hide thee from my sure revenge !

> [WEZAR *forsaken by* NEDIM, *and in ter-*
> *ror of the words he hears, drinks the*
> *phial used for poisoning his arrows.*]

> [*Enter* JERIR *and others : then* ABLA].

JERIR.

This way, good friends !

ABLA.

Dearest, my Love !—I come !—

JERIR.

What ails thee brother ?—

ABLA.

Say, where is he, where ?—

ANTAR.

Abla, art here ?—

ABLA.

Yes, Love, I heard your voice,
And I am near you : say, you are not hurt ?—
Or that I dreamed !

ANTAR.

Sweet Love,—'tis nothing, still !
Some secret coward reptile from the reeds
Hath set his treacherous sting upon my thigh.—
Aye, help me, Love ; the wound hath been so swift
That, like the sharpest hurts which children have,
Bidding the tardiest tears,—it doth forget
To bleed.

ABLA.

O God in Heaven, be kind to Me !—

JERIR.

Go Abla, Beauty,—and you gentle friends,
And lead him hence with ye ;—but as for Me,
I'll glut these eyes,—dye red this tingling steel
With the fell traitor's blood !—Was it from thence ?—

ANTAR.

Aye, due across the stream.—Come Abla, child !

[*Jerir plunges into the river : Antar goes to the tent*].

G

Scene III.   Within the tent.

ANTAR.

Be not so grave sweet Friends at this my hurt :
And by no means despair !   Though to you all
I may display how cruel Fortune plays,
Who, through unnumbered fights and frequent perils,
E'en to the lips of Danger held me safe,
As if the deadliest airs were impotent
While I stood by : yet do behold how here
(Using the hidden worm to spoil the oak,
When with one flash of levin it were dead),
A trivial shaft She has let pass at me,—
Not as it were upon the radiant noon,
Where-on a nice Consideration aims,
And fools itself by error ;—but mark you,—
Along the viewless hollow of the night
Where life itself meseems allured the dart ;
Though it has failed the targe !—

AMRU.

                              An 'twere thy life,
We vow revenge on this accursèd deed !
See now, our JERIR had no fruitless toil !
Something at least, they seem to bring behind.
Give me a lantern !—

                         [*Enter* JERIR *and others.*]

ANTAR.

                          Moments lend more light !
What Fortune guided you, my valiant One ?—
                              [*Aside to* ABLA].
I feel a sudden coldness creep within me !
That shawl from thy dear shoulders, for this once !

JERIR.

My gentle brother, proof is there—without !—
When, after a fond battle with the stream,

(Whereon blind Darkness seemed so falsely strayed
It clung about my head that I scarce knew
Whether the stream or It most made me strive),—
I took the sandy reach and staggered out,—
Scarce one bare pace on dry-land had I gone,—
But, as a wanderer in some spring-grown wood
Stumbles mayhap athwart some hidden bole
Felled in hoar winter, tho' yet unremoved,—
I tripped, (at first I deemed, on sleeping beasts,)
And with my out-stretched hand I found a man,
Breathless, but warm ; new-fallen,—without wound ;
Lying full length like an up-rooted pine !—
And while I watched, pale-peering o'er her shroud
The risen Moon o'ersicklied all his face.
Behold, yon dripping coverlet conceals
The clue to all !— [*They bring in the corpse and the bow.*]
                    The arrows were all gone !

ANTAR.

O ABLA, Sweet : Ah, Heaven, forgive my soul !—

ABLA.

Dear gentle Love, as you now gaze at me,
You seem to steal an iciness like Death's
From that dread face forlorn !—

ANTAR.

                    Ah ! Abla,—Dove,—
Whose tender love is still my Morning-star
'Neath whose unwavering resplendency,
As battles with advantage of the sun,—
My Life's reverses have been duly met,
And I have vanquished them : O true sweet Love,
I would not aim so bitter-sweet a word
At Thee, were't not Affection's self conspires,
And forces me through my preventant Will
To quench for Aye, Hope's unpermitted flame ;—

That is the corpse of WEZAR, Carad's son,
Whose vile revenge, look you, out-reaches me
In his last arrow : fatallest of foes !—
Among all mine the only one I feared ;
Though most within my will.—[*All horror-struck*].

ABLA.

        Is that the same ?
My cousin WEZAR ?—Nay, it cannot be !—
Can comely Youth become so grossly changed ?—
Its proper bound take on such loathed extreme ?—
My cousin surely must have died ere now ?
His name has been so long among the dead.—

ANTAR.

Take him, my friends : he should not linger here !—
While you who knew him not, give me your ears ! ! !—
Thrice at my feet cowered he upon the dust,
Wrested from off his steed ; and every time
I did restore his freedom forfeited :
For he was bold, and valiant in assault ;
And where he battled, warriors fled like birds ;
Yet like a craven, envious of just fame—
Unmindful for the liberty he swayed
From my good-will,—he tried three several times
Under the suit of Love to deal me Death ;
Whence Accident—true friend of Innocence,
And my own witless error, me with-held.
Such is the Fiend attends a licensed heart !—
Twice I reprieved, and briefly set him free :
For he was grand in battle.—What I spared,
Was one small Hero-part ; but inasmuch
As, saving that, he was a murderous wretch,—
Hateful in Heaven's eye, and a curse to Man,—
I did command that those redeemless orbs
Which, as two evil planets led him on
To things insufferable, should be destroyed ;

And thus he found those poor effectless lids.
Then they related—those who did the act,—
What demon seemed to rage within the man :
For when but quit those thralling torturers
That gave him darkness all this side the Grave,
He cursed my soul and laughed out blasphemies,
Rheuming upon their faces. This wretch thought
To live—nay, flourish, on my dire perdition,
Making my death an April for his soul :
But Death hath ta'en him too.—We should rejoice
If but a twinkling we outlive a foe :
For his off-taking proveth Death our friend.

ABLA.

Yet who puts Hope thus far from you, dear Love,
To whom with Me scarce one brief hour ago
She was a sweet inveterate friend ?—Alas !—
Does a mere shaft-wound thus unmettle you,—
A little harmless flower of a wound ?—
You, who in Danger's brunt deride the lance
Lifted to kill—the pitiless imminent sword ?—
How puny is this hurt !—I do not think
But ere to-morrow's eve it will be closed.

ANTAR.

Closed with a little bribing silvery sand
To keep Death in her new-found dwelling-place,—
To lock her from my friends !—Aye, my sweet Love,
Too soon I fall the bright wings of our Hope,
But not the soaring pinions of true love !
Tho' on the bitter dawn-rise yet to-come
I fold the plumes of Valour to their rest.
That shaft was dipped in Death !

ABLA.

            Ah ! say not that !
Can Night so quickly then, close out sweet Day ?

Can Night so quickly then, close out sweet Day ?—
Then Abla never smiles on Earth again !—
Life is forlorn, and all her love—discrowned !

ANTAR.

Mark you the curses of that fallen lip :
The fettered mischief of that sullen brow
Where secret thunder rages !·—E'en the ear,
Like to the deadly snake that charmers use,
Bemocks with daintiness each gentle sound.—

[*Turning to Abla.*]

Did not the clouds up-gather to our song ?—
So will come Death, my sweet sweet faithful Love,
Upon the matins of the little birds !
I see her misty train upon the breeze :
And for her ensign, mark !—a wisp of cloud
Torn from the quivering side of some dark Storm !
The light of Life rebukes her sable robes :
No question moves her pale imperious lips ;
Her eyes are of the lustre of the sun ! ! !—
Abla, me-thinks like Thine :—and on her mouth
I see a bud-rose blanched—a fading pleasure,—

[ABLA *folds her arms around him.*]

A maiden's love-song !—Aye, it is as white
As these small hawthorn-flowers around my neck !
I feel acold !—   *   *   *   *   *   *

Then when She saw his thoughts were wandering,
And He spake less by reason than by dreams,
Like to a lion's mate bereft her lord,
Abla, crying aloud in utter grief,
Spoiled her beautiful raiment with hot tears :
Her pale cheeks too like lilies of the night,
Shone with the burning sorrow ; while around,
The flickering tent-light lit each face forlorn,
And flashed upon her Chief's unreasoned eyes.

But when his words were noised along the camp,
Shrill sounds of woe aroused the breath-less night,
And wild lament of maidens rent the air,—
Soiling their beautied hair with dismal dust,—
Smiting their bosoms.—-But the child of Malik,
Remembering all the suffering of her tribe
Broke into passionate grief beside her Spouse.—
   " Race of Abs, thy Glory is paled for ever !
Dark too are all thy days : for thy Sun is fallen !
Souls illustrious mourn for our matchless Hero,
           Valorous Antar !

" Heaven is dark. The light of his sword is faded :
All our foes drank death at his hands like water.
Lakes of blood made He for the lapping lions,
           Slaying the Tyrants.

" Aye ! but his Love was sweeter to me than honey :
Loyaller He than the best of the race of mortals,
           Nobler in counsel !—

" Down the midnight in the torturing silence,
Lonely I met the glorious eyes that loved me :
Saw the straight bright throat and the resolute features
           Gleam thro' the darkness !—

" Heard his splendid voice in the depth of anguish
.Open sweetly, hovering o'er my senses,
Winged with deathless Love:—Ah ! what can comfort
           Desolate Abla ?"

PART IV.

   So all that dreadful night one fierce lament
Gathered under the dark distempered clouds
Where the grey Moon stole weirdly. But when Morn
Mounting in glorious armour o'er the heights,
Swift as an eagle, scared the wolfish mists,

Antar burning amid fierce agonies,
Said to his weeping friends,—"Let no vain tears
" O valiant well-loved comrades, dim your eyes :
" Under an equal law God rules us all !
" Who may withdraw himself from Destiny ?"—
Then leaning softlier round to Abla, said :—
" Belovèd child, alas ! Now I being gone,
" Who will protect your honour, or your life ?
" Well know I that the tribe of Banu-Abs,
" Stricken of this my strength and these my arms,
" Will be o'er-whelmed.   Arabia cries aloud
" For vengeance on it.   Yea, none but as I
" Can save you from the pangs of slavery ;
" Amer and Zeid-el-Khail alone of all,—
" Of all the warriors who wear horse-tail helms,
" Who fought for us at widowing Jelilel
" Can now defend your honour and the tribe ;
" Choose then of these to offer him your hand !
" Withal, to pass the desert safelier,
" To gain your kinsmen,—thus I counsel you :
" Take Abjar, my good steed, and in my arms
" Let your fair limbs be clad ! fear no attack :
" Bear yourself as beseems.   Deign no salute :
" For a sight of the horse of Antar,—his keen sword,—
" The airiest shadow of his Indian spear,—
" E'en as a body whereon death has passed,—
" Will daunt the boldest."—
                              Then the kingly Sun
Loosed his fair armies down the distant slopes
Of high Katraneh ; while delicious breaths
Of drowsy flowers awaking to the morn
Wandered around him lying in the tent.—
For there the golden Gardener blithely strewed
His rathe especial sweets withouten stint,
Careless, like yellow ore that ancient rills

Delving a mountain-vein have huddled down,
Then drying, left aglitter in some vale.
At his own will albeit, they took him forth
Whence he might breathe and watch the smiling scene ;
So there he gave his wealth in flocks and herds
And all his fruitless booties to his friends ;—
To Abla most of all ;—there-with his gems—
[Beryl and jacinth from the Javan isles ;—
Pearls that had mooned upon the dusky breasts
Of far South Queens ; and things of carven gold
Wherein whole leaves of emerald slept inlaid,
Emblems of summer ; fragrant veils of silk
Which Khosroe bought with gems from realms remote :
And fair Sidonian tunics flower-enwrought,
With curious linens of antique device,
And many-coloured scarves and spices rare,
And jewelled cups of Shiraz, deep-embossed ;
With peacock-plumes and sheeny tiger-skins :]—
For he was princely, and he loved her much.
But Abla knew not, though she heard him speak !
Dark night had fastened on her wondering lids
And like a lady in dream with dolorous heart
She stood, awhisper, while her keen tears came,
Rolling in torrents down her faded cheeks,
Gleaming the ebon fringes of her eyes
That lightning'd back her soul's light.

                        Then more soft,
Turning to Amru, his belovèd friend :—
" Amru, my Soul's Delight, estrangeless friend !
" Sweet youth on whom the un-noting world should dote,
" I prithee get thee back to Aneyzeh,
" Fruitful, with many wells,—where all thy tribe
" Shine with their fair pavilions, like the stars.
"Speak not my parting : tell not One thereof !
" How-be what time the earlier breezes blow,

" And the fair breathing bosom of the Spring
" Kindles thy yearning soul with high desire,
" Then Amru,—then call Thou my face to mind,—
" With all those tender thoughts of glorious Flower,
" That married our twin souls in peace and war !
" Think not of me as One who 'neath the soil
" Lies with incestuous Change,—a Work less loved
" By Him who rules, than by the sensual worm
" That garners nothing, but degrades and spoils
" The pride of Nature !—But think Thou of Me
" As of one who never smote a helpless foe,
" Nor ever did a noble deed dispraise :
" Aye, rather loved to make a foe his friend."—

    Then he embraced him : and in silence deep,
Amru, with hidden eyes, went faltering forth,
And the blithe breezes caught his sable curls ;
While passing to his charger with a sigh—
One manful groan, heard but of those anear,—
His Morning-star swept westward on the wind,
And he was seen no more.
                  Then through a line
Of mounted warriors glittering with straight spears,
Abla in all the armour of her Spouse,—
Fair as the moon upon the midnight heaven,—
Came slowly, sitting astride that ebon Steed :
Like to a single lily on the stream !
In her right hand she kept the dreaded lance
That shone like Sirius or Canopus' light,—
Or the calm planet lit with many moons :—
And at her side hung low that mighty sword
The smith had wrought of old in Samarcand.
So to the litter whilom used by Her,
His trusty friends helped Antar ; and he smiled.

PART V

As when upon some June-day by the sea,
With never a least white fleck of wandering cloud
To darken the lit flowers along our path,
On the horizon a soft argent line,
Like endless visionary cliff, appears
Gliding unevenly, though surely, on ;—
So, having lost the emerald river-banks,
Across the bright interminable sand
Marched laden bulls and tedious camel-herds, ·
And serried spears that shimmered over them :
Aloof all these, like a cloud-ruling Goddess,
Gleaming in orient state, imperial,
On the slim courser coloured like the Night,
Rode Abla ; while behind her, Jerir went ;
And in the sumptuous litter, camel-borne,
Lay ANTAR, dreaming deathward as he slept.

But far along the border of the plain,
Lacing with silver all the sapphire sky,
A myriad tents, ere-then unseen of them,
Broke the wide solitude : and magic-wise
An hundred horsemen, rapid as gazelles,
Hurried athwart the mystic desert-line,
Till reining sharp his steed, the Leader cried :—
" ANTAR it is ! Alas ! Behold his arms,
" And Abla's queenly litter, and the steed !—
" Let us in haste for our lives ! Alack-a-day !
" His wrath will be upon us : let us flee ! "—
Whereat they wheeled and fled ; though one old Sheikh
Adept in sifting signs of mystery,
Rallied some round and spake these words to them :

" Friends, it is Antar's lance, his sword, his helm,—
" His nimble courser coloured like the Night ;—
" But who in That sees his so princely amien,
" Straight as the lordliest cedar of the grove ?—
" May-be some wound or fitful malady
" With-held his mounting !—Aye, it might be so :
" And Abjar carries for disguise some friend
" Clad in his lustrous arms ?"—None nathëless
Dared to creep near : but following arear
Like craven vultures awed by yieldless prey,
Trusted some token of the truth to see.

Like a sweet rose that hungering Frost enjoys;
Leaving it all out-wearied to the morn,
Abla sat bent, and pale with sleeplessness,
Until as noontide lemed down fiercelier,
Turning to liquid flame the level plain,—
The heavy lance so drooped her dainty arm
That as she rode, it furrowed in the sand.
Then, as an eagle on its vantage-rock
Espies with thirsty vision the least spot
That stirs within its calm encircling realm,—
With his well-practised eyes that hoary Sheikh
Well-marked that lance entrammeled by the sand,
And becked assurance to his faltering friends,
Till at his token, like a shoreward wave,
Couching their spears they swept athwart the line—

Then like the royal roar that fills the pause
Fore-led by chatter of apes and jungle-birds,—
Or thunderous sea-cave when a billow strikes,—
Awaking 'mid shrill cries and thud of hoofs,
And bellowing foemen, and the clash of arms
Antar uplifting gave a mighty cry,
And arching up his wild, insatiate eyes
Turned and looked forth, and while he rose they fled,

Clinging for life along their hurtling steeds,
And vanished in a whirling cope of sand ;—
Yelling in terror : " Evil day ! alas !
" Antar yet lives, to lure us to our doom
" That he may learn which clan out-braves him most."-

Thus in despite that bony-cheeked old man
Whose craftier hints had hailed them to attack,—
Despite entreaties, promises, rewards,
They fled like silly hares that men surprise :
Or as a flight of curlews that uprise,
And urging from one sportsman. fall a prey !
Though he cried out and taunted, toiled and cursed,
Dubbing them lustless eunuchs till some turned ;
Then reining, frenzied, mid their sweltering jades,
He bade them pry along the desert-verge
To watch those winding files.   " In sooth," said he,
" Antar is sorely wounded, or some hurt
" Having befallen him, he woos repose ?
" Let us now follow, and take note afar ! "—

But Antar, though the slakeless fire or pain
Burned on relentlessly, with faint slow voice
Bade them return his arms that Abla wore.
So they unlaced the helmet from her head
And loosed the steely plates that bound her breast ;
And took the heavy lance and iron shield ;
Then after that, they laid her, trembling, pale,
Like to a tristful little aspen-leaf,—
In the soft glittering litter as He rose.

Once more in his loved armour being arrayed
(Tenfold beloved since She had borne its weight—
For Love increaseth with each burden shared !)—
He faltered fondly to caress his steed—
Striking its hoofs there, on the printless sand !

But one that loved him, drawing near, exclaimed :—
" Antar, for us hast thou fought long and well ;
" To-day then truly we will fight for Thee.
" Prithee treasure thy still remaining strength,
" Not, reckless, cast it from thee at one throw !"

But ANTAR said, " My friends, I hear your words ;
" Yet verily, if I won aught for ye,
" Advance : I will defend you till the end ;
" And ere to-night we may with Peace repose :
" Antar yet aids you : though his waning words
" Must soon grow soundless in the last long Sleep !"—
Therefore they went, and silently obeyed.

PART VI.

What time the Night rose o'er the looming hills,
The Desert heard no sound save flocks remote,
And tinkling camel-bells and neigh of steeds
That wound among the tufted silver dunes ;
And the full-moon fleckless above the twilight,
Spangled the ivory litter where She lay ;—
Glimmered on His dark armour ; then more bright
Rippled it weirdly down his trembled spear
And casually fired his frosting eyes.
While softly by him roamed delicious gales,
Freighted with balmiest virtue from those flowers
That breathed of Love ;—till in the narrowing glen,—
As when some Zephyr mars a peerless Rose,
Streaming its crimson treasury to the earth ;—
Or sweet rain brimming from a lotus-flower,
The Bul-bul loosed his sweetest notes of Woe
Until the stars seemed thronging there to hear.

But when they drew anear the sheltering vale,
Antar made every Chief to pass therein :
And Abla slept : nor would he mar her sleep
E'en though his face would feel her kiss no more,
Nor ever shall he hear her tender voice
Breathe out one little plaintive sweet ' farewell !'—
He waved one kiss above her pallid lids—
Quite closed like Night's white roses, from the stars,—
And bade them bear her softly down the vale,
Lulling her with the melody she loved ;
While slowly he returned,—oft looking back !—

So when they faded from his wistful gaze,
And only faint, receding music came,
He reined his charger,—loftily shining there,
Like a weird sea-ward rock that sailors fear.

Wherefore those lithe keen spies that held arear,
Stayed marvelling afar what he would do ;
Though some in terror crept-off, whispering low :—
" Let us escape beneath the hindering night !
" For he but counsels to destroy us all !"—
But in contentious accent spake that Sage :—
" None but the godless counsel cowardice !
" This movelessness, I ween, is Death's own sleep,
" Haply he is now dead ?—Knew ye his ways ?—
" When ownèd He the onslaught of a foe ?
" Did not he glean his foes as men glean corn ?—
" Or as the Northwind rains the Asoka-bloom ?—
" Aye, like an eagle, would have dropped on us,
" Plucking this armour bloodied from our limbs.
" Forward then, yarely ! or at least remain
" Till dawn resolve us an my word be true ?"—

Therefore all night they shivered sleeplessly,
Till taunting Morn out-spread his eager wings,

Sweeping obsequious Darkness from the hills,
And mocked the crew of quiverers where they stood,
Bathing with glory all the desolate arms,
And ebon Abjar 'neath his bright dead Lord !

   Thus, like a pack of lean and agued wolves
Snuffling around a lion as he preys,
Anxiously eyeing the carcase from afar,
These prowlers stood, and shook like feeble reeds
When shuddering Dawn creeps greyly up the stream :
Till their wan leader, tendering no more words,
Slily took foot ; and couching his thin spear,
Stole near the moveless steed with crafty stride :
Then crawling snake-wise pricked so suddenly,
That Abjar with one fearful fiery leap
Darkened across the desert, letting fall,
E'en like a glorious tower earthquake-rocked, —
His matchless master on the sparkling sand ;
And all his armour rang among the hills;—
Even as the clash a thousand cymbals give !

   Whereon they rushed to him in one accord,
Gazing amazedly for dearth of words ;
Scanning the One at whom Arabia quaked,
There, grandly still, upon the troubled sand,—
His face upturned upon the golden morn !
So long looked they and praised his peerless form,
His tangled hair aglitter in the breeze,—
His brow so full of counsel and command,
And tender temples of triumphant eyes
That seemed but shining proudlier under Death—
Even as the Night shines when the Sun has gone !

   Whilas they stood there, on exultant wings
An eagle soared above them ; then fled on,
Tipped with resplendent morning, to the plains,—
As marking there, no common son of Man !

So they unloosed his arms and took his lance ;
Yet, honouring a foe so right-renowned,
Hollowed the sand thereby and laid him down ;
And when they went aloof, their hoary chief
Knelt down beside him, glimmering with tears,
Muttering :—" Honour, O Hero, be to Thee ;
" Living, the true protector of the Wronged,
" And in thy death their best defender still !
" May kindly dews refresh this hallowed sand
" Where We, the Desert-sons, now lay thee down,—
" Erst foes, now friends ! Sweet peace be unto Thee !"

There then, he rests ; and all They sought their tents.

THE RETURN OF TASSO TO SORRENTO.

A POEM IN TWO PARTS.

NAPLES.

The shore by the Castel Dell' Ovo : a boat being got ready.

TASSO.

Once more sweet Heaven ; upon this golden shore !
And there, beyond, across the azure bay,
E'en like a faery coast dim-seen in dreams,
I view the low dull cliff,—the ridge behind,—
The guardian headland brow-bound with white mist,
Dark-under-streaked with many-sounding rills :
And there are olive-groves,—and lemons There,
Girdling the peaceful village,—looked upon
May-be e'en now, by eyes that live to love me ?—

[He gets into the boat].

Each distant sail meseems a silvery sprite
Hailing me homeward !—Thou dear Shore, adieu !
Farewell sweet Naples !—and thou time-worn Keep
Whose ancient hall our Giotto .did adorn
In days of eld, right guest for sapient King,—

That now invaded by the frolic waves
Dost take thy colour from the charmèd clouds
That limn their mystic likeness on yon sea !—
How much opposed, O Heaven, to those stern towers
That frown like storming tyrants on the face
Of him Ferrara greets !—For who on those
Can gaze unvisioning Parisina's fate,
And tender Hugo's ?—Hence with thee, dread picture !
The kindliest hint of thee would mar this scene.
For now we skim aslant the free, bright sea
And all our steepy Isles are dreaming round,
Like gathered seamew sleeping on the wave.—
There, to the northward, Pozzuoli lies,—
That shrines the Pride of Mantua and the World :
A little gold-dust from the stream of Time.
There too, Boccaccio's soul broke all aflame,—
With passionate song and merriment inspired,—
Even as a bird that knows the Winter gone
And pours its rapture to the uncaptived world.
Now sunward Monte D'Auro, at whose feet
Castellamare sleeps,—untires his head,
And shews intrenchant, like a Warrior tall
Planted upon the amethystine morn :—
Monte St. Angelo too,—But what are these,
Or aught that noblest poets ever praised,—
Weighed with one balmy breath from my Sorrento ?—
Well-clepèd by some Dorian bard of Eld
" The Syren ! "—since to me she is in deed :—
She is a bounteous Goddess high-enthroned ;—
Her footstool is this choral sapphire sea ;
And her aërial ministers the Hills,
Stand in embattled panoply around,—
As if attent to her least utterance !
But yond I see, sweet Heaven ! above the cliff,

Cornelia's house—the cot where I was born
What time uprose the rathe anemonies,—
And sweet Narcissus on each grassy cliff
Let from his golden cups the twinkling spice,—
Enraptured at the busy-whispering waves
That hive within the grey rocks far below   .
Like weary bees thick-laden from the isles.
Ah yes, the house I see where dwelt a Maid,—
The queenliest flower in all our countryside,
Throned in a realm of Beauty, and beloved,
And modest in her beauty's innocence :
The rainbow is more conscious of less charm,—
For Her attractions are as infinite,—
As various (tho' more sweetly loveable),
As there are changing beauties in the skies.—
A sister and inestimable Friend,
Whose old affection in these fingered scraps
I treasure near the beating of my heart,
As if it were the Child of my delight·
Sleeping to my heart's music—made for It.—·
How I do love thee, sweet Cornelia !
Yet things have changed us, sister, since that day ·
When on yon shore, I kissed thee, and thine eyes
Glittered with helpless tears against the dawn
That looked as cheerless as our olives do
When loitering breezes creep beneath their leaves ;—
Methought, poor child, I should not see thee more :
But Fate, the leavening chamberlain of Life
Out from behind Its arras drags me forth
And thro' the hall of Freedom leads me Home ! ·

    I think she should not know me in this guise ?—
Misdeem me some poor shepherd ?—In the street
Our merrier urchins will make mock of me,—

Style me a Tuscan reptile, or the like?—
Yet having sweet persuasion in his soul,
What stings a man can bear!—What-ho, the breeze
Has wafted us too far!—this is the cape
Where Statius says Friend Pollius had a villa
Dainty, incomparable;—Look where it lies!—
The Sea has mined it: dynasties of Storm
Have battled it for fourteen-hundred years,
So that at last it crumbles down the rocks
Strewing them as 'twere a tree with fruit o'er-ripe:
And yet so many glorious fragments live
That Fancy, the sweet mason of the Senses,
With easy labour builds it there again!

Here good friends, let me land!—Adieu! Adieu!—

> [*He leaps out of the boat on to the rock, and
> vanishes up the path of the cliff*].

THE HOUSE OF THE TASSOS AT SORRENTO.

[*Cornelia his sister, and Julietta her friend*].

JULIETTA.

Cornelia Sweet, you seem not well to-day!
Come to the terrace: for the sea wind blows!
The children have gone playing to the shore;
And look:—a fairy boat I see out there
Skimming along the blue bay like a dove
That spreads its pinions on the morning rise
And toil-less aims towards its native home.
Aye, 'tis a morning full of May-delights,—
And will you grieve upon it?

CORNELIA.

O Julietta,
If all the sweets of all the various months,
Heaped in their beauty, were now offered me,
I do not think but that I should quite refuse them !
And as to this mild breeze you'd have me breathe,—
It has blown long ; yet never blew me Good !
I know it ere the casement lets it in.
It never strikes the dainty poise of sense
So even but it sways with opposites,
Making each quality of humour chide :—
First I am courting ; then I straightway hate it .
Then having fled it,—forthwith wish me back !
I would that heaven would bid it blow no more.
It mocks me when my heart will bear no mock.
Thus what we might love, may yet prove our Foe !

JULIETTA.

Yet do not rail at that which hears thee not ?—
That were a contradiction worse than all :
Yea, 'twere more foolish than to love a statue !
For that being loved, Imagination's wand
Might conjure motion from its plastic stiffness,--
Endow it with the rosy hues of life :—
So that insooth it might give sweet assent !—
But this mere recreant wind is reasonless,
And has besides, nor eyes, nor shape, nor hue !—
You have too many hopes that all of them
Should in so brief a space be quite fulfilled ;
Besides, might spend your trouble, telling it :
Yet that you will not, and so seem more cold,--
Even from Me reserving more and more !

CORNELIA.

Dearest, I never hid a thought from You !
'Tis cruel thus to chide me !—What I have
Is not a multitude of hopes or pains
(And they at worst, were busy company) ;
But one lone sorrow 'tis, and ah—one Hope !

JULIETTA.

Then is't a widowed sorrow : mine is maiden !—
It cannot be Torquato's absence still ?—

CORNELIA.

Ah yes, Julietta ; and from my dim thoughts
That haunt like phantoms, there is no escape.
Hark you, and mark the snakes that kill my sleep !—
Last night I dreamed he stood beside my bed,
Heavy and worn with troubles; and he sang.
O it would make the tears rush down the cheeks
Of savage beasts, I think, to hear his song !—
And while the sweet voice singing sighed away
Into a mournful echo,—Lo, there came
Two felon jailers—one each side of him,
And dragged him roughly whither I could not see :—
And all my fruitless rage—(this too, I dreamed—
Which worked within the wound upon my heart),—
Induced such impotence within my limbs,
That though my mind's hand tore their murderous eyes,
My body stirred not, and they went unharmed !
But there—'twas but a dream : I trust no more.
Though people say such dreams foretoken Truths !

JULIETTA.

I'll not believe it : 'tis mere fantasy !
Dreams are such reasonless imaginings,

That mix all colours, shapes, localities
Upon the plastic palette of the brain,·
Making us rough-cast poets.

CORNELIA.

That word Poet
To me is music ! yet I scarcely know
All that it means ; although beloved Torquato
Has now for full five years by men and Kings
Proclaimed been the fourth among our bards !—
If to call things by their accepted names,—
Or (to bespite the world), be all one seems,
Doth compass the word Poet,—I am one !
Yet am not I upon the lips of kings.—

JULIETTA.

Nay, nay, Cornelia ! But to call each thing
By any name save that which is its name ;—
To cheat the very bareness of its title
Out of simplicity, and to create afresh
Is, you will say, the contrary in all
To that you heard called Poet : nathëless
I have known them that did this, too, called Poets.
Yet to be what one looks befits not you :
For you are lovelier darling, than you seem ;
Though you be Beauty's self !—And as to that,—
A King's lips !—why I trust the next, Unseen,
Will prove himself to have more worthy ones,
On which yourself, your name, and Love, may live !—
For I have learned long rolls of Emperors
And Kings, and Popes and Princes numberless,
Whose good exceptions aped rare Accidents :
So that I deemed far better, Men had been
Ruling themselves than so to be misgoverned !

CORNELIA.

Still mocking !—Yet once I did reverence Kings
And Rulers of all kinds.   But since this Beast,
The wolfish Este binds my brother's Will,
I cherish bitterest hatred to them all ;
And had these eyes but lightning in their brightness,
I would uptear and agonise them so,
That their wild shrieks were anthems in my ears :—
Their desperate torment—like delicious strains !
Little they know what sisters we have here !—

JULIETTA.   [*Half aside*].

Little they know the peril of their deeds,
Or they would bless their lot by night and day
For every league betwixt them and Sorrento !—

CORNELIA.

Ah, you like all the rest do choose to rail !—
I shall believe in Nothing soon from spite
At having long believed in everything !

JULIETTA.

Ah what is, that ?—Cornelia do you hear ?—
A man is singing dainty songs to you :—
But not by any means in praise of Love.

CORNELIA.

O yes, look how the children tease him, see,
Pulling his tattered cloak, now here, now there ;—
And mark,—he only gives them kindly smiles !
The old men come !—He stops ! they drive the lads,
And ask him for more songs—

JULIETTA.

                    Now see : he looks !

CORNELIA.

Ah ! My heart beats !

JULIETTA.
Nay, but why ?—

CORNELIA.
Great Heaven ! ! !
Am I distraught ?—possessed ?—'Tis He ! 'tis He ! !
O my Torquato—   [*She rushes out and embraces him*].

JULIETTA.   [*Aside*].
What ?—come back again ?—
This seeming beggar ?—Sure the Soul is mad !

CORNELIA.
[*Returning with Tasso, who whispers significantly*].
Belovèd one, my only one !—my poet !—
          [*Great laughter of old men without*].

1ST OLD MAN.
Well, 'tis a quaintly business !—O those ladies ! ! !—
I too, had once a voice ; but my reward
Came not so quickly ?

2ND OLD MAN.
No, nor in that coin !

1ST OLD MAN.
A plague upon the fellow !—Aye—a plague !—
You copious Crook-face,—O you—

2ND OLD MAN.
Hi !   Hi ! !   Hi ! ! !
          [*Exit mocking*].

[*Within*]   TASSO.
Nay sister, hide my name !—E'en from Thyself ! !—
In this disguise I came—escaped, I say :
I could not bear my life, so fled ; yet fear
The Duke may trap me like a thievish fox

If he but scent my name : wherefore this garb,
To which I do entreat your colder show
Of merest courtesy when others pass !

CORNELIA.

Aye, anything to keep you with me still !
Now, dear Julietta, mark this gentleman,—
And swear, if any ask you of his name,
                              [*Julietta bringing some wine*].
He hails from Bergamo—on our affairs.—
If pressed,—he is our Cousin :—but at home,
Here, in his father's house, 'twixt you and me,
He is my own Torquato !—   [*Embraces him*].

JULIETTA.   [*Aside*].
                    Wonderful !
It is an odd wind that first turns the milk, [*Going out*].
And vexes all the milkers ;—then transforms
A weeping widow to a merry minx !

I'll go and fetch an orange for him now,—
While she dries up his tears ! He must be tired !— .
The children will be coming back in glee,
At having seen that boat dragged up the shore !
Hark, at their voices now !—And will he love them ?—
Ah ! he will love them for their Mother's sake !—

TASSO.   [*appearing above*].
Nay ! He will love the children—for *themselves* !

FINIS.

[Sorrento, 1881]

Lycon, an ocean awes your venturous feet
Which never feels the calm that loves our shore,
Your Clime too, never bids a sweet flower blow
Sheer thro' the sterile Winter's iron bound!
Therefore, my friend, delights beknown to me
Are being upstored to please your leisure-time.

My days are spent along the trancèd shore
That looks on Capri and Inarimé,—
Down rocks the wild-bee never honeycombed,—
Great silent stones that hold the ancient storms,—
That listen to the sea's unvarying tale.
O you would love to watch this tideless bay,
Whereunder all the sea-flowers breathe their love
In changes un-beheld of blind Mankind:
Even our innovations cannot worst them!

Yet e'en the secrets, friend, of Time himself
Are drawn away and kissed from him by flowers:
These are the garlands which we bribe him with.
Here may you see the dainty Celandine,
Like to a golden Pilot of the winds
Watching the dawn-rise from each sunny cape:
And none among your mirthless folk could count
The charms that deck our loved Anemone,

Our fair elected Empress of the Spring !—
The Rainbow knows not Her variety !
Then random Stock empurples every rift,
Daring the fall ; and whispering Maidenhair
Waves in its steep recess with amorous winds
Dispensing all its moonlit infant rain
To the far-down Acanthus lovingly :
Sceptering our headlands too, behold the Pines
That intermarry their imperial boughs,
And sound like mighty harps along our sea ;
While dreaming waves fall softly to their song
In showers of sunniest pearl !—You could not count
Our olives, or our fig-trees, or our vines :
The lamps of heaven are not so numberless !
At this sweet season, Lemon-flowers ablow
Enrapture all the air of all the hours,
Insatiate of the narrow-bounded day ;
Tho' many a bud sleeps yet against the sun,
Still in its captive white, like Infancy
Enshrouding all that will unfold Divine,—
To bless the eye that views it !—Had I time,
I might a myriad other beauties name,
To trance your vision with !—alas, the hour
When goats to milking must be driven, is come,
And all their wantonings at each green thing
Adown the path will see the Sun to sleep :
Lycon, my friend, take Fancy's flight to Me ;—
And may thy dreams be happy as my days !

IDYLL II.

The Muse of this fair morning led me Here
Through those melodious woods,—among the vines:
I know how I came !—but Sun and Shade,
Like rival syrens, wildly drew me on
Over the ivied rocks, on lawns aslant,
Till this torn glen displays the listening Sea ;
And ceaseless o'er the dimly-creeping shore,
Yon over-peering mountain, dragon-like,
Belches aloft its heavy-labouring breath,
As if in throes of lethàl agony,—
Back to the mightier dreamy Appenines,
Whose Kingly heads do chide its sullied white
For seeming so to mock them on their thrones ;
And villas, all ascatter like the stars,
Enlace with silver all the cradled hills ;—
While merrily assembling on the bay,
Like pearly seamew, glide the merchant-ships
As if enamoured of the wanton Spring.

Here in a dewless hollow, lichen-stained,
The colour of Time's locks, I sit adream,—
Hearkening the mazy glen-rill tumbling down,
Admiring purple star-flowers quivering soft,

On the grey edge around the dark, straight depth :
And in the murmurous air uprising here,
Narciss out-sweetens e'en his usual self,
Honeying the very Heaven ;—while joyously,
Chameleons gambol o'er my moveless feet,
Like imps of flaming emerald, unalarmed.
Haply they call me friend ?   Then Philomel,
Yearning with unsung melody, drops by
Into a spicy thicket near above ;
Whence singing she will lull the drowsy noon
As if she heralded the Day of Love.
O who shall tell the glory of this place
Wisdom is barren if it bears not Love !

AT MAGGIORE.

I.

Grim storms have a white net enwoven
    Over the giant crags :
Through clefts, of the Earthquake cloven,
    A lone cloud angrily drags :
Yet us-ward the breezes that die light,
    Enwaft from the roseate hills,
The hallowing incense of twilight
    Entoned by a thousand rills
With rivers of song from the soul of the Bird that the
    Night's heart fills.

II.

While Evening comes down from her highlands
    To whisper at Night's dim door.
Night's voice are the leaves on the islands
    . And ripple of waves on the shore.—
O who would not swoon at the closes
    Of songs that she sings in her bowers,—
Her lips being soft as the Rose's
    And sweet as those ivory flowers
That bare the bright soul of their love to embosom the
    raven Hours ?

III.

Or who will take note of the Morning,
 How urgent so-ever he be,
Arrayed in his utmost adorning
 As Lord of the land and the sea,—
When Night in her infinite glories,
 Eternal, ingrained and inlaid,—
Alights from elysian stories
 Of Heaven, in whispering shade,
To beguile sweet Earth of her woe that the Morning
  made ?—

IV.

Ah ! Night, thou Mistress of pleasure !
 O Mother of dreams that flee !
O Queen of delight-without-measure !
 Thou Goddess of Sleep and the Sea !
Our songs ever feebly confessing
 The splendour of things that are free
Are laid at thy feet for thy blessing,
 A gift, alas, nothing to Thee !
Let thy wings lower lightly upon us thro' Time that
  now Is and to-Be !—

1879.

THE FURNACE OR THE MINT?

GLOWING, fiery, like divinest
Nectar from ambrosial flagons,—
(New rain in a golden poppy),—
In the crucible more noble
Than in graven coins of Nations,
Seems to me the glorious metal!—
So too, from the Soul that gloweth
With Love's stainless flame, the purest,
Sweet Thoughts do shine out more perfect
Than from books of cunning Thinkers!

WHERE the broken heather blooms,
                    O come with me !
Far beneath the billow booms
From a cave where noonday glooms
                    Under the sea :

While the woodbine's odour weddeth
        With our pleasure ; and the bee
        Earns from flowers his golden fee,
And the virgin Wild-rose sheddeth
        All her treasure sweet and free.
                    Love, come with me !—

PAST, like Beauty's first impression
    Has this sweet Day from our eyes
Aye, and holiest intercession
    Cannot make it rearise.
Only, Love, its radiant vision
    Someday stealeth unforseen :—
Then the Present's dull partition
    Will once more its charm en-screen

Mist and solemn Night together
  O er the twilight hills are speeding,
Like two birds of equal feather
  Flying onward, nothing heeding
Till they sing aloof ill-weather.

Blue be the morning ! full of singing
  All the fragrant cypress-trees,
Whither we, Love, shall be winging
  On the next enfavouring breeze !

I<small>F</small> we cross the stormy sea,
  Still this mystic power enfolds us !
If to the land of Death we'd flee,—
  Wondrous sweetly it with-holds us
And (who knows?) this unseen tether
  Binding Man against his will,—
Out of sight, past flight of feather
  If he fly may bind him still ?—

I <small>GIVE</small> Thee a Book of Sages :
    Title—gone ; and dull of cover !
Yet deep life inspires its pages,
    Uttering Music for its Lover.
      When storm then hides thy calm,—
      Like high melodious psalm,
    May its old spirit hover
Softly o'er thy wearied Soul ;
    Stay thy tumult of Despairs ;
Make thy faltering courage Whole :—
    Turn to Joy thy load of Cares !

GREYLY o'er the leaden waves
   The banded clouds of Night are driving
Silent, swiftly, like mute slaves
   Who for Freedom's love are striving
To out-speed the Despot's might
On the secret wings of night.
   Darker than the plumes of raven
Looms a distant storm behind
In the armoury of the wind.—
   Many a glorious ship its haven
In the deep the Morn will find!—

THOU art ringed with the locks
  Of the 'Tempest, O Isle ;
And the roar of it mocks
  Thy light innocent smile.
The fires of its eyes are illuming thy capes ;
The mouth of its anger like Hell's mouth gapes.
Yet I ween, tho' the Night may enshroud thee with
    sorrow,
Thou'lt gladden our hearts with thy beauty to-
    morrow !

THE TIDE OF THE FLOWERS.

UNDER blithe melodious April
Lifts the magic tide of flowers
Rippling on with white and violet,
Purple, azure, green and golden,—
All in ceaseless undulation ;
While Her sweet voice laughs above it.—
Then it steeps the lips of Summer !
Autumn cometh: lo! it faileth —
And at Winter-time remaineth
Leafless waste for lonely Man !—

A DESERT-PICTURE.

BROKEN lie the spears around Him :--
Harmless now the widowing arrow !
Dim are the Warrior's eyes to twilight !
Like two flowers his lids are closing :
The pale sand all his life is lapping.
While the Starlight takes his spirit
As a green lawn in the spring-tide
From the breeze receives a blossom.—

All the wilderness in silence
Lies beneath the breathless heaven ;
While the low moon, like an onyx,
Dimly a weird rock illumines,
Where the fowls of Death are watching ;
And beneath them, in the shadows,
Silent, motionless, majestic,—
Waits the velvet-footed Lion !

SONNET.

How stale and profitless the poor words seem
    That meet to do soft honour to Thy name !—
Their early freshness soiled by Time's dull stream ;
    Their youthly fire fall'n spiritless and tame !—
Yet,—as sweet Music oft the fanc sublimes,—
    I fondly use Thy name ; (O not in vain
The soul unto the body of my rhymes !)—
    Prone to entice fled Glory back again !
For as the Indian diver carves a shell
    In Budda's image, which the deeps empearl,—
So in my heart, hath Love with hallowing spell
    Engraved Thy beauty, * *, my sweet Girl ;—
And if Fate lifts me up, or lays me low,
Here, in my inmost,—here for Aye, art Thou.

I.

Lo, the Light, and the Sea his sister
Playing afar in the windless hollows !
She left dream when twilight kissed her :
He—what time the grey-dawn follows
The flying feet of the vanished Night ;
    And the livelong day
    They prattle and play
Where the Land, her Lover, lies down in his might.

II.

SEE how Light's fingers, the fragrant Breezes,
    Have buried the great grey form in flowers,
    Save at his feet, where the Sea's keen Showers
Hurt and dishearten each flower that seizes
    Blindly, unbidden, the limbs of her choice :—
    Ah, many the golden
    Delight, unbeholden
Of rapturous eyes, that recoils at her voice !—
For her sisters, her brothers, her lovers that woo,
    Are giants all ; to whom no God saith,—
As unto us cometh :—" Your days are few :
" My Sea, though tender, is terrible too !—
    " Her words are soft as the Summer's breath :—
    " But her kiss—is Death ! "

Lynton.

STORMILY, stormily,
Pennon and standard,
Gather the thunderclouds
Angrily sweeping
Down o'er the mountain-brows
Into our valley !
Sweetly the Valley gleams
Giving back smile for frown
Clear from its open stream,
Fair from its golden field,—
To the Oppressor !—

Callander.

WAR.

ALL is hushed within the village,
  Where so late a savage Flood
Strewed its pleading lane with pillage,
  Tinged its golden fields with blood.
O'er the little kirk yet hovers
  Thick the dark rage of the Wronger :
  Marriage-bells ring There no longer
And in Death's arms lie the Lovers.

A VISION OF DEATH.

His pen is of iron :
He signs the warrant
For a thousand
Tears,—a torrent
Of unheeded sighs !
Broken cries
And hopeless hearts
Spring from his path,
By glen and strath,—
Where-from He parts :—
Where-to He hies !
For Man,—poor Thing !—
Just views Him King ;
His tyrant-frown,—
His spectral crown,—
Then falleth down
A-withering.

SONNET.

To You who have been long in Cities pent
  Whose poisonous veils of smoke (Misfortune's hue)
Enshroud, or quite blot out—as was not meant
  By God,—your sky, when first He made it blue,
Would Ye know where to pass your leisure-day
  And own sweet respite from your sunless toil ?—
There is a spot retirèd from a bay
  Where Devon spreads the bounties of her soil ;
Gay flowers cluster on the village-walls ;
  Lithe grasses wave along the chequered hills ;
And there are whispering woods and merry falls,
  And eke God's-acre where the mavis trills.
O, if Ye have a care to know the same,
Come westward ! Berrynarbor is its name.

WILD-FLOWER LANE.

In the narrow upland lanes,
  Which the elder-trees embower,
Throughout summer, Day-light wanes
  Long ere His appointed hour.
There the close leaves tune the rains
  When the wildest Thunder-shower
To it's quick-past wrath attains ;

While the little country-girls
Nip the Nettle's purple whorls,
Basil too, and Bryony,—
And the blue-eye Succory
That, for freak, hath leapt the hedge
From the golden barley's edge.
And from these they weave, I trow,
Garlands fit for Beauty's brow :
Till the merry Yaffingale
Tells anew his joyous tale.

CEREUS GRANDIFLORUS.

THUS the flower of noble Talent
Differs from the flower of Genius,—
Sun and shower may e'er command it
As the busy world desireth.
But the glorious flower of Genius
Strangely spreads its kingly blossom
Half-foreseen, upon some midnight,
And the Centuries encircling,
Gaze with wondering lids upon it ;
For, alas, too soon it fadeth !—

DILLETANTI AND ARTIST.

THIN wine in a gilded goblet !
  Heigho, works of Dilletanti !!
Aye, but work of one true Artist?—
  Tumblers-full of old Chianti !!!

K

THE LAST TEAR.

HEIGHO for a tiny tear!—
A little, silent, mortal tear—
Shaken from a Snowdrop bright
By the breeze of Death and Night.
Morning with his golden spear
Did contend against Them here,
Till Love with passion-streaming eyes
Looked around in dread surmise,
And beheld her Little One
Gone to sleep against the sun !

SONG

Coy little Golden-Head,
  Why, why so sad ?—
Did'st thou in doubt or dread
  Part frae thy lad ?—
  Sigh to the west-wind ;
  Sing to the flowers !
  Alone thro' the hours
They'll bid thee look glad.
Blithe little golden-Head,
  O be not sad !

A NEW YEAR'S GREETING.

O'er a massy cliff, imperilled
By the winds and waves of era,
Calmly from her throne of Sapphire,
Sweetly from the hall of Twilight,
Love's own star hath smiled on me ;
So my Friend, I pray that Hope's light
May as calmly,—still more sweetly,
Glow, while life remains, on Thee !

I

O come here ! see Lady Summer,
  Through the lattice of leaves where she sups,
And her page the merry hummer
  Dallying round her nectar-cups !
Little elves attend her wishes :
  While her mate—the dainty dove,
From all flowers derives her ~~daintier~~ dishes :
  And her wines are made of Love.
Honeyed flowers without number
  Shed around a golden blaze :
'Tis a place where Grief may slumber,
  And Delight might end his days.

Birds for Love of Her are sighing :
  Fallow-deer peep thro' her bowers :
With her eyes the stars are vying :
  With her hair—the Mary-flowers.
On the ear bright tales of travel
  From the moon-lit brooks arise ;
Where amid the maddening ravel
  Of the glistening water-flies,
Fallen Fox-glove-bells are drifting,
  Drowned with elfin melodies.

"LOOK HERE ON THIS PICTURE;—AND ON THIS!"

II

Far from pride of place and greed-dom,
   Here one fills the soul with bliss;
And with warm, enraptured freedom,
   Trembles Nature to a kiss.
Here no honest eye is misted
   With cross-purpose, doubtful, dark:
Aye, my Friend, Here naught is twisted,—
   Save the old thorn-trees in the park.
There the Human potter's varnish
   Cracks, revealing all the clay:
There a Soul of gold might tarnish,
   And its scutcheon rub away!
There, whatever nook be chosen,
   North-winds on your heart must blow:
There the Spirit's wings are frozen,
   And its nest is filled with snow.—
Here no picture cold and clinic
   Need philosophers be giving:—
Nor, thank Heaven, need prurient Cynic
   Drivel out, "Is life worth living?"—

Clovelly.

THE HERMITAGE OF KANDU.

A HINDU LEGEND.

[*According to Brahmanic mythology, Indra may lose his rank as Lord of the secondary Deities, and be compelled, by irresistible Destiny, to surrender to any Penitent who, by mortifying austerities, shall surpass the merit he himself had previously achieved.*]

Calm as the royal Sun above the dream
Of Asian summer's noon,—amid the play
Of chasing Irises,—irradiant
With gems that inter-wreathed his lotus-crown,—
Fair as the star that sings the birth of Night,
Throned on a slope in Swerga, Indra sat,
Supreme, alone !—while to his raptured ears,
Welled from the glimmering paradise below,—
Like the mild odours of the opening flowers
That dally with the soft, rebukeless air,—
Divisions of such sweet-attempered sound
That mortals had they twenty earthly lives,
Would hazard each to hear the honied least !—
For there, among the many fragrant bowers,
By inter-arching glades and emerald lawns,
Spirits, the fair perfection of their times
In worldly faithfulness, exalted now,
In company of Devas heavenly-born,
Bright with the soul of Beauty, sang aloud
In glorious symphony, divine-compact,—
Smiling in soft unweariable Bliss.

But while the mighty God attent thereto,
His matchless realm regarded,—on the air,
Even as the frolic lisp of willow-leaves
When the blithe May-winds kiss their Love, the Stream,
A band of shining Spirits, like the spray
Of bright salute a lost orb wafts to Earth
Seen in full glory of the living sun,—
Or dewy plumes some wounded eagle falls
Cleaving the fiery air at morning-rise,—
Swimming through balmy haze, alighted soft
Upon a pearlen terrace near their Sire :
Yet saddened in their looks with such a grief
As mortal jealousy gives Love,—Him thus addressed :—

" O Sire resplendent, deathless, ever-young,
" Giver of beauty, hearken to our plaint!
" For on the little Earth, we mark, dismayed,
" A lonely hermit, who, unsatisfied
" With radiant hope of earning Bliss with Us,—
" Reward sufficient for the best of Men,—
" Aspires by bitter dole and joy denied,
" With self-affliction limitless, to rap,
" Or leastly, twinlike—share Thy sovran throne.
" Such fond conceit can fasting move in Man,
" Turning his else too-practic mind to air
" And wandering fire, till He at last o'erleaps
" The brink of Sense to find no footing more
" Save in the happier grave or here in Heaven.
" Indra, we love Thee ; hearken to our prayer !"

Then like a wailing sound they died away
Into their lowlier paradise.—There-on,
Flushed with new fear, Lord Indra rose erect,
And with a tender voice that thrilled the stars,
Summoned the fairest Beauty of the place—

The nymph Mureela, soft as nestling dove;—
Who, without sound, as dew on morning-leaves,
Uprising on a bow of light intense,
Drew to the joyous presence of her Sire ;—
To whom a spirit held a beryl-cup
Brimming with sunniest wine, Amrita hight,
Sweeter than any Lotus of the streams,—
Whose rosy drops fell glittering through Space,
And touching our gross Earth, froze into gems,—
Saphires and rubies, opals full of Fate !
Anon, at her persuasive loveliness
Amazed anew, the gentle God began :—

" O Beauty, take the wings of Morning hence :
" Like to a song, float down the nether sky,
" And light thou on the glorious River's bank,—
" Gomati, where the ripe fruit drifts away :—
" Then through the woodland urge thy random steps :
" Find out for me this holy Eremite,
" And by his sense en-mesh him : spare thou not
" Thy subtlest power to mar his steadfastness !
" One breath of thy enchantment will unhasp
" The stoutest cords that Conscience twines in Man.
" This One would leap the common bound of Good,
" And scorning our sweet Garden, share with Me
" The everlasting throne where-on I sit."

There-at the lily-nymph afraid, replied :—
" Mighty Divinity, whose glorious voice
" To hear, is sure obedience,—even as flowers
" Obey the sovereign sun-beam,—I depart
" Ungladly, sorrowing from Thee : lest from Him,
" Shrewdly fore-judging me, some thralling curse
" Be all my greeting, and ashamed I flee —
" Foiled in the very blossom of my charge !

" Great Sire, with lowly tears I Thee entreat,
" Some wiser nymph, more eloquent of charm,
" May mock the peril of this dread emprise ?"—

To whose meek words, that fell upon his ears
Like the retiring Summer's evening voice,
The consort of Satîhi thus rejoined :—
" O weep not Child of Beauty !—nay, arise,
" And hie thee like the breath of Dawn itself :
" And I will grant thee Zephyr and sweet Spring
" As helpmates meet to further thy desire !"—

So, with a cloud of sweetness, new-exhaled,
The gentle Beauty vanished : while the song
Of loitering Zephyr trembled all the air.

PART II.

Even as a flight of bees that float and whirl
And fade amid a scarf of sunny mist,
What-time the awakening gardens pour aloft
Sweet breath of flowers,—so those Syrens flew ;
Till the far-murmuring waters of the world
Seemed to attune their flight ; while through a veil
Of swift-dispersing vapour they beheld
An emerald forest as a garden fair,
All-overstrewn with inter-twining flowers
Trembling ablaze; and in blithe symphony
Out-sweetening all the song that River made
Winding with dreamy falls adown its glens —
Blue as the tranquil sky,—incomparable
Save to their own Nandana ever-fair
Which laps with blissful wave the fragrant roots
Of flowers that never fail in Paradise !—

(For in the swirling eddies of the stream,—
O token of the tender changing Earth !—
Fair legions of sweet flowers swept along
On to the bitter seaward silently.)
So there-beside, upon a mossy knoll
Purple with tubed Rattle, loved of bees,
Soft as a cloud,—and many another bud
(Till now restrained in cool funereal shade,)
That broke abloom by reason of her touch,
The Goddess and her light companions lit,
Pleasing the air then blest with hope of May.
But Spring and Zephyr softly took their way
Under the morning-glory, leaving Her
(Reluctant half, to bid farewell), alone.
But when she knew them gone, Herself advanced
Amid the soft-contending Light and Shade
That,—as two sun-birds o'er some welling flower
Whose flashing nectar trickles down unsipped
Amid their strife,—about her lovely limbs
Full sweetly quarrelled ; while, among the leaves
Conspiring, with new rapture birds unseen
Poured their quick ecstacies, and flitted on,
Tuning Her footsteps, heralding their Queen.
But when She drew beside a gleaming pool
Whereon the azure height with myriad Loves
Of billowed inter-linking clouds displayed
Herself the lily-lustre of them all,—
They flamed around her like an opal-shower;
And in the forest-depth the Koil sang.

Thus to her dainty, sweet-surprisèd eyes,
Each brake where haply cowered a brinded pard,
Each harsher note where-with the woodland woke,
Shorn of its natural terror, soft appeared,—
As if Devotion's dwelling made it so,

Dispensing influence divine, like Love !
Thus like the Waterlily at her feet
That peered in snowiest beauty o'er the pool,
Mureela stood and lulled the birds to sleep—
Wearied with too much bliss.
      Then Zephyr breathed,
Sipping the topmost flowers as he passed,—
Thrilling their balmy leaves ; while cheerful Spring
Put forth his sweetest strength, and hung the air
With unsuspected fragrance, quickening, wild,
Resembling that of Heaven.
      Then Kandù,—
Steeped in his trembling lips with wonderment,—
His bosom wildly flushed with strange desires,
Hearing such music,—rushed in frantic wise
Out of a thorny brake : yet when his eyes
Weeping devoutly, through the mist of tears
Beheld the forest quivering with delight
Round the immortal Nymph that like the moon,
Friendless, and fair, in leafy twilight stood,
His lean, starved reason fled,—his saintly care
Like breaking frost, dissolved ; and Memory,
The plastic monitor of Conscience, failed,
Leaving him aidless,—victim to the Gods :
But rallying his lost, disordered zeal
That strove, how vainly ! through his fire-bright eyes,
He coldly bade Her tell him how She came,
Conjuring by his Vows : how-beit his words
Seemed like a mist that sunrise turns to dew
And lingeringly fell like Love to Her,
Who, lifting up her plaintive eyes, replied :—
" In me, O stranger, but a lowly maid
" Strayed from the River and my loving friends
" Not far away, hast Thou found gathering flowers :
" Yet not afraid came I along these glades,

"So sweetly civil did the forest seem,—
" As if the higher Gods might tenant it,
" Breathing delightful peace and love around !
" O blame not me that I invade your bowers,
" Who in such innocence thus had never come,
" Immodest, unadorned, had I but dreamed
" Aught but the vestal Heaven had eyes to see.
" And reason with ! "—

       Howbeit approached, amazed,
He took her dainty, unreluctant hand,
And kissed the glory of her flowing hair:
But at the touch, the influent fire of Youth
Flamed thro' the bursting husk about his heart
And freed the rosy seed imprisoned there,
And flashed his feasting eyes, and fired his soul
Till lonesome, heart to heart, She knew his love ;
While the great Sun went down on their delight,
And Champac-breathing Night, I ween,
Blsssed them beneath the branches green !

Part III.

But Swerga heard loud peremptory Song :
For thus the lesser Gods do taste a joy
Over aspiring Mortals once dismayed !
Wherefore Success, the Spendthrift of great Minds,
Most drains their rich resources at best use ;—
And like large debt a wise Realm owes itself,
Argues a brisk, strong and trust-worthy life.
The better Man excels the meaner God !—
The least of perfect daisies in the shade
Out-glories beauty cankered in a rose !

So too, the tiniest planet, simple-bright,
Borrowing, may-be, his garment from the Sun,
His royal and obeyed true master,—wings
A course more temperate and less peril-fraught
Than comets charactered with strange extremes.
Therefore I leave the Gods—to pity Man.
For We are effortful : They need no aid :
Yet wither Us with scorn from crown to sole,
When Failure's levin blasts us from within,—
Heaping perdition on our ruined heads
Until the toppling pile supports a throne
From which beneath their sated brows they smile,
Wearing the leaves of Shame for victor's bays.
If greatest Gods indeed are greater men,—
Also the worst Gods are debasèd men :—
The ringless coin of Earth, made light at first,
Against full-weighted and shrill-sounding Gold :—
Yet mostly, men prefer the counterfeit !—

Now liberal Spring wrought such emboldening change
By cunning sorcery on that poor Youth,—
Turning each alien frown to Love's own smile ;
Each wan void cheek bedimpling with Desire ;—
His caved breast—like the golden-fronted Sun,
Changing each local grief to general joy,
That Heaven's ambassadress found a blither friend
In whom she conquered than she knew in Heaven ;
(For Love the Spirit, loves the earthly form
As being more plastic to its tender will ;
Thus flattering with self-likeness its Creator !
Love knows but Love, and imitates itself),—
Therefore the giddy months fled by like days,—
Liker than chosen pearls on silken thread,
Or lilies that engarland Beauty's brow,—
For very love of Him ; and never a thought

Of all those blisses that the High-Gods boast
In other heaven, did overtake her joy.
So in delight unending, ever-new,—
(For true Love never cloys : to the soul's eye
Being various most where Reason sees no change) :—
They sweetly-unreluctant there abode ;
Till one cool evening lowering Winterward,—
[Alas that mean minds by success grow hard
And play with victim Love as tigers do !]—
She him beheld, his brow in sore perplex,
Chiding with silent scorn his dainty lips,—
His fingers tangled in his long bright hair
Therefore She slily sought him of his will,
Hoping to win some curious thought from him !
But with rebukeful voice, each word distinct
As any crystal, He ;—" Nay, see you not
" The shadows fast descending ?—I must hence,
" And fail not of my evening-sacrifice :
" The great moths are abroad : the firefly stirs,
" Making dim circles on the dewing grass :
" With shrill cicalas all the depths resound ;
" And the quick stars are crowding out the sky ; —
Looking, unmoved, as tho' he knew Her not
More nearly than the cold fair stars beyond !
Then the Immortal tears arose afire,
In her sad flower-like eyes of sweet regard,
Marking the bitter change : yet She did say,—
" Dear Love, this day is but a little thing !
" To One who loves, there seem less stars than days.
" The load of Time is thrown so much before
" By never-wearying Hope and well-poised Love—
" Reflection has no need to turn his head.
" Prithee, what worth has this so casual day
" Above those days un-meted into months
" Which Heaven has sweetly for our joy displayed ?—

" Or who on High will note one offering less ?"—
Then he like one awaking from a dream,
With eyelids distant, in amaze, replied,—
" Nay! for Enchanting One, this very morn
" Into my thorny grot I Thee received,
" Meeting Thee lonely by yon crystal pool,
"Standing uncomforted, a wanderer, lone ?—

And She,—" But how forbid my lips a smile
" When since the morn you speak of, hence have sped
" Beneath the sun ten honey-laden months,
" Storing for us their nectared memories ! —
" Hast Thou forgotten all our Joy so soon ?—
" Thy vowed adorement unto Me, alone,—
O Faithless One? who for thy thankless sake,
Was All in All, aye, more All to Thee ?—

" Alluring Beauty, is it truth indeed,—
" Or but thy merry play to daze my sense ?
" For but a single day has fled ; in-sooth
" Thou speakest of some other one than I!
"I am a hermit ; and my lonely care
" With sacrifices and keen penitence
" To build Reward to-come an ivory throne
" Equal with Indra's, and to share his realm !
" Can it so be that I, the stainless Man,
" So morioned with hard Truth—so hedged and armed
" With iron thoughts and steely constancy
" Have fallen by a May-day gossamer,
" Blown, like a painted bubble, random-wise ?—
" And dost thou laugh at me ?—Undone !—Forlorn !!
"She leaves me !—And the sky grows dark above !"—

Then from an ashen pall, on his bright head
A flood of rain descended pitiless,

Splitting the thready plantain-leaves around ;
While through the moonlit forest fronting him,
He saw the lovely Goddess fading fast,
Between her blithe companions : so he ran
To over-take them : crying out in grief; .
Till rushing blindly to the River's brink
He nigh out-sped them : but the quarried bank
Felt his sharp step, and undergave his feet,
So that he fell upon the sudden stream
And with the eddying flower was borne away :
But They uprose into the silvery height ;
And sat in Swerga ere the morning-light !—

FINIS

LONDON :

S. AND J. BRAWN, PRINTERS, 13, GATE STREET, HIGH HOLBORN, W.C.